Chapter 1

Breakfast at Aunt Lucy's. Oh yeah! It didn't get much better than that. It was only French toast, but she made it like no one else could. I obviously wasn't the only one who thought so because the twins were there too, and they were dropping crumbs all over the carpet.

My name is Jill Gooder, and I'm a private investigator. I'd taken over the family business after my adoptive father died. My life had become much more complicated when I'd discovered that I was a witch.

I divided my time between Washbridge, which was in the human world, and Candlefield, which was home to all manner of supernaturals (sups for short). That's where I was this morning, with Aunt Lucy and my cousins, Amber and Pearl—witches all of us.

"Girls! How many times do I have to tell you about dropping crumbs?" Aunt Lucy yelled.

"Sorry, Mum," the twins chorused. They didn't look particularly sorry as they each took another bite, and made even more mess.

"Why can't you two use a plate?" Aunt Lucy scowled at them. "If Jill can do it, why can't you?"

As soon as Aunt Lucy had disappeared back into the kitchen, Amber mocked, "If Jill can do it, why can't you?"

"Jill's such a good girl," Pearl said, and then the two of them dissolved into giggles.

I did the adult thing, and stuck my tongue out at them. I was with Aunt Lucy on this one. I hated it when my adoptive sister, Kathy, and her kids descended on my

nice, clean, tidy flat and left their mess behind.

The twins had given up on their hair dying exploits, and had both reverted to their natural colour of ginger—for now at least.

"How's Cuppy C doing?" I glanced at my empty plate, and wondered if asking for a third slice of toast would border on greedy.

Cuppy C was the twins' cake shop and tea room.

"Takings are up." Amber was half way through *her* third slice.

"Business is good, but we've had a few problems with one of our cupcake suppliers," Amber said, then turned to the kitchen. "Mum, can I have another slice, please?"

"Three is enough for anyone."

Amber pouted.

"What's the problem with the cakes?" I asked.

"We've been getting damaged cupcakes in our deliveries for a while now," Pearl said.

"Why don't you change supplier?"

"We use more than one already, but Christy's cakes are by far and away the best."

"Yeah." Amber was eyeing her sister's last half slice of toast. "Mrs Christy is super nice. She can't understand why they're having this problem. It's like someone is deliberately sabotaging her. We've promised to stick with her for now, but if it keeps happening, we may have to reconsider."

"Beryl Christie?" Aunt Lucy had rejoined us—her gaze surveying the trail of crumbs which led to the twins. "She and I go way back."

"That's one of the reasons we don't want to drop her," Amber said. "Hopefully, she'll get things sorted out."

"Hey, Mum. Have you told Jill your big news?"

Was that a clever ploy by Pearl to distract her mother from the crumbs? If so, it seemed to work.

"I'd hardly call it big news."

"What's happened?" I said.

"Tell her, Mum," Amber pressed.

"It's the first ever Candlefield Baking Competition this weekend," Aunt Lucy said.

"Mum will win it hands down." Amber edged away from the crumbs.

"No contest." Pearl finished the last of her toast.

"I haven't decided if I'm going to enter." Aunt Lucy joined me on the sofa. "I've got a lot on."

"You have to enter," I said. "We can give you a hand around the house if you need time to focus on the baking, can't we girls?"

The twins looked at me like I'd lost my mind.

"Yeah, I guess," Pearl said, somewhat half-heartedly.

"I suppose so." Amber sighed.

"Thanks, Jill." Aunt Lucy beamed, and then turned to the girls. "I'm overwhelmed by your enthusiasm. You can start by cleaning up that trail of crumbs."

The twins exchanged a glance.

"She was talking to you."

"No, she was talking to *you*."

Ten minutes, and one prolonged argument later, the twins took it in turns to vacuum the carpet while Aunt Lucy and I escaped into the kitchen.

"Those girls will be the death of me." She grinned.

"Seriously though, you really should enter the competition."

"Make sure your professional indemnity insurance is up to date first," Grandma said. Neither of us had heard her come in over the sound of the vacuum. "You'll need it to cover all the claims for food poisoning."

"Good morning, Mother." Aunt Lucy clenched her fists. "How good of you to honour us with your presence."

"I'm only saying. I wouldn't want you to bankrupt the family."

"Grandma," I said much louder than I'd intended. "Aunt Lucy is a fabulous baker."

"Thank you, dear." Aunt Lucy smiled at me.

"What's for breakfast?" Grandma took a seat at the kitchen table. "And what's that damn noise?"

The woman was unbelievable. If I'd been Aunt Lucy, I'd have told her to sling her hook.

"French toast."

"I suppose that will have to do." Grandma sighed. "Jill, go and tell whoever is making that noise to stop before I turn them into a termite."

Any excuse to escape.

I gestured to Pearl to kill the vacuum.

"What?" she shouted.

"Grandma's here. Turn it off!"

She still couldn't hear what I was saying, so I walked across the room, and pressed the 'off' switch.

"Grandma's here." I pointed to the kitchen.

Pearl nodded.

"Let's go," Amber said in a whisper.

The three of us slipped out the back door, through the garden and onto the street.

"Is Grandma in a bad mood?" Pearl asked, as we made

our way to Cuppy C.

"When is she *not* in a bad mood? She really annoys me when she criticises your mum's cooking."

"I know. It's not like *she* can cook. Have you seen that vegetable soup she makes?"

"The one that looks like it's made from dead toads?" I laughed.

"Smells like them too."

"I don't know why Mum puts up with it," Amber said. "She should tell Grandma to make her own meals if she doesn't like her cooking."

Pearl laughed. "Like *you* would dare say that."

"I didn't say I'd say it, but Mum totally should."

"Do you think Aunt Lucy will enter the competition?" I said.

"She's more likely to now that Grandma has riled her."

Was it possible Grandma had said what she did for that reason? Nah, she was just an evil witch.

"What do you think her chances of winning will be?"

"Hard to say. There are some good bakers in Candlefield, but a lot of them rely on magic. The competition is strictly no magic allowed — that should favour Mum."

Cuppy C was already open for business. The twins had taken on and trained staff who could now effectively run the business when they weren't there.

"How's things?" Amber called to the young woman behind the cake counter.

"Another damaged delivery."

"Christy's?"

The young woman nodded. "I had to bin a quarter of them."

The twins turned to one another. "We have to do something," Pearl said.

"I know, but Mum won't like it."

"We can't let things carry on like this."

"Would you like me to look into it?" I offered. "Maybe I can find out what's going on?"

"Would you?" Amber said.

"Sure, no problem."

We'd just examined the latest Christy's consignment. The boxes showed no sign of damage, but several of the cupcakes had been squashed.

"When will you be seeing Drake again?" Amber asked.

"I'm not sure I will be."

"Why not?" Pearl looked as surprised as her sister by my response. "I thought you two had really hit it off."

"We did, I guess."

"So what's wrong?" Amber said.

"If I tell you, you have to promise not to repeat it."

"We promise."

"Cross your hearts?"

They both did.

"After you'd shown the wedding photos to Daze, she took me to one side and told me that she knew Drake. It seems she arrested him some years ago."

I'd been out with Drake a couple of times—nothing serious, but I'd enjoyed his company. I'd actually begun to think it might be leading somewhere when Daze had told me that she'd arrested him some years before. Daze's real name was Daisy Flowers. She was a super sup, and an RR, which stood for Rogue Retriever. She brought rogue supernaturals back from the human world.

"Drake was a Rogue?" Amber looked surprised.

I nodded.

"What did he do?"

"I don't know. I suppose I should have asked Daze, but I was too shocked at the time."

"Have you said anything to him?"

I shook my head. "I've been kind of avoiding him since then. I don't really know what I'm going to do."

"Bummer!" Pearl said.

My thoughts exactly.

Before returning to Washbridge, I called in at Christy's bakery. The small industrial unit on the outskirts of Candlefield had a bright red, pink and white sign with a picture of a cupcake on it. The twins had phoned ahead, so Beryl Christy was expecting me.

"Mrs Christy?"

"Call me Beryl." She looked to be about the same age as Aunt Lucy, and shared the same quirkiness in dress and glasses. "You must be the new witch in town. I've heard a lot about you. Do come in."

Beryl gave me a quick guided tour. The premises were spotlessly clean, and the whole operation seemed to run like clockwork. Several times, she offered me the opportunity to sample the goods, but I somehow managed to resist. Twenty minutes later, I was in her office—cup of tea in hand.

"I feel terrible about all of this," she said. "I don't want to lose the twins' business, but I don't blame them for being annoyed. It isn't only them either, it's happened with some of my other customers too."

"Do you have any idea what might be causing the

problem? Have you had a change of staff?"

"No, nothing like that. Most of my staff have been with me for years. I'm stumped. I can't help but feel that it's deliberate though—someone is trying to sabotage my business."

"Maybe I can help, if you'll allow me to."

"How?"

"I work as a private investigator in the human world."

"I'm not sure I need a private investigator."

"The twins think you do."

"I couldn't afford to pay you."

"I'll accept cupcakes in lieu of payment. If they're anywhere near as good as Aunt Lucy says, then it'll be worth it."

"What would you do exactly?"

"I'd like to start by working undercover at the bakery."

"I suppose that would be okay. I'll see what I can arrange."

When I got back to Cuppy C, the twins were on a tea break. Did those girls actually ever do any work? I joined them at their favourite window table.

"Beryl Christy is a sweetheart," I said.

"That's why we don't want to drop her. Did you come up with anything?" Pearl was cutting a strawberry cupcake in half. She had a theory that if she ate it in two halves, it was fewer calories—don't ask.

"Give me a chance. I'm going to work there undercover."

"Ooh, how exciting." Amber clapped her hands. "Like a spy?"

"Yeah, something like that. It'll be a couple of days before I can get started though."

Pearl took a bite of the other half of her reduced-calorie cupcake. "Me and Amber are going clothes shopping later. Do you want to join us?"

"No, thanks. I have to get back to Washbridge. What's the occasion, anyway?" As if they needed one.

They giggled. They giggled a lot.

"School reunion dance." Amber could barely contain her excitement.

"And you actually want to go?" The idea of being reunited with my school friends—and I use the term loosely—was my idea of hell.

"Of course we do."

"We can't wait. It'll be brill."

"How often do they hold them?"

"This is the first one since we left. It's going to be fantastic to see everyone again."

"Are William and Alan looking forward to it?"

The twins were both engaged. Amber to William, a werewolf; Pearl to Alan, a vampire.

"They can't go," Pearl said. "Only those who attended the school can go."

"No partners allowed?" I asked.

"No." The twins exchanged a glance. "Well, that's what we've told them. We don't want them there—we want to meet up with old friends. Anyway, they'd only be bored."

"Old friends, eh?" I was beginning to smell a rat. "Any *particular* old friends?"

"No."

"Of course not."

The twins were terrible liars.

"There's a strange man in your office," Mrs V said.

"Strange how?"

"You'll see."

The strange man was dressed in a floral shirt, lime green trousers and flip flops. His glasses were all the colours of the rainbow.

"Over there, I see glass, and chrome. Lots of chrome," he said. "Velvet for the curtains. Dark blue."

"Excuse me!" I said.

"He pirouetted around to face me. "Who are you? Can't you see I'm busy? You've interrupted my flow."

"What exactly are you doing here?"

"I'm re-imagining this space. I'm thinking maybe cyber chic with a hint of Paris."

Either I was still asleep or the local coffee shop had put something strange in my latte.

Winky beckoned me to one side, and whispered, "This is Maurice. The man is a genius."

"What's he doing here?"

"He's going to give the office a makeover."

Over my dead body. I glared at Winky. "Excuse me, Morris," I said.

"My name is pronounced Maurice—like Chevalier—not Morris. Maurice Montage."

"Well, Monsieur Montage." I gave it my best French accent, which if I'm honest was more Grimsby than Paris. "I'm Mademoiselle Jill Gooder, and this is my office."

"Pleasure to meet you." He took my hand and kissed it. "This office has such potential. You were so right to call me in. The sooner we get rid of this—" he waved his hand around the room, "the better."

"I didn't call you in."

"Your secretary then?"

"No it was—" I looked down at Winky.

"Yes?" Maurice Montage said.

"It was—err—I mean—that's to say—I guess I did contact you. I must have forgotten."

What else was I supposed to say? I could hardly tell Monsieur Montage that he'd been called in by my cat. Not unless I wanted the men in white coats to appear and cart me away. Instead, I spent an excruciating hour listening to Maurice's vision for the office.

"I can have this place transformed in a matter of weeks," he said when the ordeal finally came to an end.

"Great." I turned to Winky and whispered, "No salmon for you ever again."

"I'll let you have a quotation in writing within the next three days," he said, as he glided out of the room.

"Can't wait." And I know just where I'll file it.

"I like the sound of cyber chic," Winky said.

Chapter 2

"Today, I have a special treat for the three of you," Grandma said.

Amber looked at Pearl. Pearl looked at me. I looked at Amber. No words were necessary; each of us knew what the others were thinking.

"You could look a little happier about it." Grandma took a deep sigh. "Ungrateful girls."

It was the day of our magic lesson. They were never fun, and I was under no illusion (no pun intended) that her so called 'special treat' would be anything but a treat.

"Aren't you going to ask me what it is?"

I bit. "What's the *special treat*, Grandma?"

"I'm pleased you asked. First though, I want to pose you a question. What's the difference between magic and an illusion?"

Neither Amber nor Pearl seemed in any hurry to step in.

"An illusion is pretence," I said. "It's what magicians in the human world do. It looks like magic but it isn't really. Whereas magic, well magic is — err — magic."

"Correct, if not too eloquent."

Coming from Grandma, that was high praise.

"In today's lesson we are going to combine the two in a spell appropriately called 'illusion'. If you have studied your spell books — " She hesitated, and glanced between the three of us. As usual, the twins suddenly found their feet fascinating. I met Grandma's gaze. I'd studied this particular spell, but had yet to put it into practice.

"For the benefit of the twins then," Grandma continued. "The 'illusion' spell does exactly what its name suggests; it allows you to create an illusion. For example, if you want someone to think that the bike they are riding is actually a horse, you could use the 'illusion' spell. The bike doesn't actually turn into a horse, but to the subject of the spell, it will appear as if it has. To all other humans, the bike will still appear to be a bike. Understand?"

The three of us nodded.

"Good. One important aspect of this spell is that it will only work on humans—not on sups. You'll see why shortly. Which brings me nicely to my special treat. In order to practise the spell, we'll need some guinea pigs."

"I love guinea pigs," Amber said.

"Not real ones." Pearl laughed.

"Care to share the joke with me?" Grandma fixed the twins with her gaze.

"Nothing, Grandma. Sorry."

"As I was saying, we need humans to practise on, so we're going to take a short trip to Washbridge."

"Can we visit your shop while we're there?" Pearl asked.

"There'll be no time to visit anywhere. You're going to the human world for one reason, and one reason only. Understood?"

"Yes, Grandma."

I was about to cast a spell to transport myself to Washbridge when Grandma grabbed my arm. "We'll travel together. Take my hand."

Those horrible bony fingers?

"What are you waiting for?"

I did as I was told. Amber took my other hand; Pearl took Amber's. Once the four of us were linked together, Grandma cast her spell.

We were in a park. It took me a few moments to get my

bearings, but then I recognised it as one on the outskirts of Washbridge.

"Here." Grandma handed us each a sheet of paper which had details of the 'illusion' spell.

"Who wants to go first? Amber? Well volunteered."

Amber looked horrified. Pearl could barely hide her smirk.

Grandma took us along a path which led to a children's play area. Surely she wasn't going to have us cast the spell on children? I wouldn't have put anything past her.

She walked by the play area and stopped in front of a row of benches which looked out over a sunken garden.

"See the man over there, reading the newspaper?" Grandma said.

Amber nodded.

"Make him see a bat instead of his newspaper."

"A bat?"

Grandma nodded. Amber looked to us for reassurance, and we smiled encouragingly.

She cast the spell, and now I could see why it wouldn't work on sups. Because I was a witch, I could actually see both images—flicking back and forth. One second it looked like a newspaper, the next it looked like a bat.

"Not that kind of bat!" Grandma yelled.

I wasn't sure who looked more confused: the man who thought his newspaper had turned into a cricket bat, or Amber.

Grandma reversed the spell. The man looked a little shaken. Amber looked more than a little embarrassed.

"Your turn, Pearl. You can't possibly do any worse."

Pearl stepped forward.

"Do you see the woman lying on the grass, with the

Chihuahua next to her?"

Pearl nodded.

"I want you to make her think the Chihuahua has turned into a St Bernard."

Pearl was about to cast the spell when Grandma grabbed her arm. "You do know what a St Bernard is, don't you?"

"It's a big dog."

"Very good. I just wanted to avoid an ecclesiastical faux pas."

Pearl cast the spell. The woman jumped to her feet, and ran down the path, screaming.

Little wonder. The St Bernard looked an awful lot like a wolf from where I was standing.

"Sorry," Pearl said. "I lost focus."

Once again Grandma reversed the spell.

"So far, so bad." Grandma stared at the twins who shrank under her gaze. Then she turned to me. "Let's see what you can do."

At least I had nothing to beat.

"Do you see the young man with the Frisbee?"

I could hardly miss him in his pink tee-shirt and orange shorts.

"Make him think the Frisbee is a pizza."

"Any particular flavour or toppings?" Why did I have to be such a smart ass?

"Just do it!"

I cast the spell, and voila: one pizza.

Although I say it myself, it looked good enough to eat. Wait! Oh, no! The young man thought so too. Before I had the chance to reverse the spell, he'd bitten down hard on the Frisbee. That had to hurt.

The twins laughed. I reversed the spell as quickly as I

could. The young man checked he still had all of his teeth. Grandma turned on the twins. "Once again, Jill shows you two how it's done. You can both write me a thousand word essay entitled 'Why focus is important to a witch'."
"Grandma. That's not fair."
"Make that two thousand words."

I'd have preferred to boycott the Bugle in protest at the article they'd published in which I'd supposedly criticised the Washbridge police. Problem was, even in the internet age, it was still the best source of news for the Washbridge area. One thing the Bugle didn't lack was sensational or 'clever' front page headlines. No matter how slow the news or how humdrum the story, the Bugle could always come up with an eye-catching headline. And today's was no exception: 'Lift of Death'.
As expected, the story was low on facts, but high on sensationalism. A man had been murdered while in a lift with several other people. According to the Bugle, no one in the lift had seen the murder take place, nor had it been captured on the lift's CCTV. According to the Bugle, the police were completely 'stumped'.
No doubt a quote from an official source. The Bugle was not a big fan of the Washbridge police.

Mrs V was hard at work on a bright red sock.
"Morning, Mrs V."
She looked up from her knitting, and I could see something was amiss. "Are you okay?"
"I've had some terrible news. My sister — "
"Oh, I'm sorry. Had she been ill long?"
"She's not dead." Mrs V put her knitting down on the

desk. "She's coming to visit me."

"Don't you two get along?"

"We never have. I wish we could be more like you and Kathy."

Was she kidding? Me and Kathy get along? That would be news to both of us.

"Ever since we were kids, she's always had to get one up on me," Mrs V said. "She got better marks at school, and she was better at sports. She even got all the best boyfriends."

"I'm sure that's not true."

"It is, but I don't mind any of that. I'm used to it." She thumped the table. The last time I'd seen Mrs V so annoyed was when Winky had emptied her yarn all over the office floor. "The thing that really annoys me is that she chose to take up knitting. She only did it to spite me. It was the one thing that I was good at. She just couldn't bear it."

"I'm sure she isn't as good as you." I couldn't imagine anyone could out-knit Mrs V.

"Don't you believe it. Whatever 'G' touches turns to gold."

"G?"

"That's what I call her."

"And she calls you 'V'?"

"No, she calls me Annabel."

Obviously.

"Oh, I almost forgot," Mrs V said as I started towards my office. "I've arranged an appointment for you at ten. A Mrs Jackie Langford. She's a friend of the man who was murdered in the lift."

"I've just been reading about that in the Bugle."

"She sounded rather upset."

"Okay, thanks."

"Oh, and one more thing, Jill," Mrs V called after me. "I've found you a new accountant. He's going to pop in to see you as soon as he can."

"I can hardly wait." Accountants are always so much fun.

Winky, my one-eyed cat was stretched out on the leather sofa.

"Morning, Winky."

He shook his head.

"Cat got your tongue?" What? Come on, that was funny.

Winky sat up. He had a small notepad in his paws. He scribbled something. It read: *'I've taken a vow of silence'*.

How I resisted fist pumping the air, I don't know. But after a few minutes, curiosity got the better of me. "Why the vow of silence?"

More scribbling. *'It's a spiritual thing'*.

"Right. How long will this vow of silence last?" A week, a month. I could dream.

Winky sighed. All the scribbling was obviously wearing him out: *'24 hours'*.

Oh well. I should be grateful for small mercies.

Mrs V must have really been depressed because she didn't even offer my ten o'clock appointment a scarf or socks. Jackie Langford was middle-aged, tall and wore expensive shoes.

"Thank you for seeing me at such short notice." There was sadness in her voice.

"No problem. How can I help?"

"Are you familiar with the recent murder at Tregar

Court?"

"The murder in the lift?"

She nodded. "The victim, Alan Dennis, was a close friend of mine."

'Close friend' could mean anything—I waited for her to elaborate.

"We'd known one another for years."

Maybe she needed a prompt. "You say he was a *'close friend'*?"

"Yes, precisely that. I know there are those who believe a man and woman can never be simply friends, but that's exactly what we were to one another. He was my closest and dearest friend. We confided in one another. We helped one another."

"Never more than that?"

"No. That's why I came to see you. A *'friend'* has no standing as far as the police are concerned. If I was a relative or if we'd lived together, then maybe they'd talk to me. As it is, they won't give me the time of day. All I know is what's been reported on the TV, and in that awful local rag—whatever it's called."

"The Bugle?"

"That's the one. Insensitive reporting at its best."

No arguments from me there. "I need you to tell me everything you know. Let's start with Alan. How long had you and he been friends?"

Before she could answer, I caught a movement out of the corner of my eye. Winky had scribbled another note and was holding it aloft. Thankfully, Jackie Langford hadn't noticed. The note read: *'Need food and milk - NOW!'*

"Sorry." I stood up. "Before we get started, would you mind if I fed the cat?"

I know what you're thinking — not very professional, but if I'd ignored him, he would have kept at it, and I'd never have been able to concentrate.

"Cat?" She'd been so focussed on her own grief that she hadn't noticed Winky. "Oh, yes, I didn't see him there. He's a handsome little guy, isn't he?"

"In his own way, I guess."

Winky scribbled a note, and passed it surreptitiously to me. It read: *'I like her.'*

Once the cat was settled with his food and a saucer of milk, I got back to the case in hand. "Sorry about that. Where were we?"

"Alan was such a kind man. Such an honest man. I know people throw those terms around willy nilly, but in his case it was true. He was truly a good man and a dear friend." She wiped away a tear.

"Can you think of anyone who would want to kill him?"

She shook her head. "No one. I can't believe it could have been someone who knew him. Do you think it could have been a stranger?"

"It's always possible, but the vast majority of murders are committed by someone known to the victim. Have you been to his apartment?"

"Only on a couple of occasions. We met originally through work; we were in the same office. Then, after I changed jobs, we stayed in touch. We usually met for coffee or lunch. He'd never actually been to my house."

"Had he lived at Tregar Court long?"

"Five years, perhaps a little longer. It must be incredibly expensive to live there. Have you seen the development?"

I shook my head. Although I'd never visited Tregar, I was well aware that properties in that post code were way above my pay grade.

"They're very exclusive," she said.

"When was the last time you saw Alan?"

"Three weeks ago. We met every two or three weeks on average. We'd arranged to meet for coffee that day —"

Her tears began to flow — I really should have invested in a box of tissues.

"Would you like a drink? Tea? Coffee?"

"No, thanks." Luckily she'd had the foresight to bring her own tissues. "I'm okay."

"You said you used to work with Alan. What did he do for a living?"

"He was an accountant."

Perhaps my ex accountant, Mr Robert Roberts, had been right to quit the profession. It was obviously more dangerous than I'd realised.

"Not any old accountant," she said. "He worked exclusively for wealthy, private clients."

"A few disreputable types among them?"

"Oh no!" She sprang to his defence. "Like I said, Alan was a thoroughly honest man. He would never have taken on a client who he knew was breaking the law. It simply wasn't in his nature."

We talked for another thirty minutes. Or at least, Jackie talked — I mostly listened. It was impossible not to draw the conclusion that she'd been in love with Alan Dennis.

"Anything else you can tell me about him? Anything at all?"

"I don't think so. Only that he was very much a creature of habit. He always went to the same restaurants, and ordered the same food. He even wore the same suit to work every day."

She must have seen the horrified look on my face because she continued, "I don't mean the exact same suit. He must have owned half a dozen—all identical. He did the same with ties and shoes. I used to tease him about it, but he couldn't see the problem. He insisted it made perfect sense to stick with something he liked." She managed a weak smile. "Men, eh?"

'*She was nice.*' Winky scribbled after she had left.
"Let's hope I can help her." I walked through to Mrs V who still looked glum. "Can you try to make me an appointment to see Detective Maxwell?"
For some reason, that seemed to put a smile on her face. What was it with her and Kathy? They seemed determined to pair me up with Detective Jack Maxwell. He'd only recently transferred to Washbridge, and to say we hadn't immediately hit it off would have been something of an understatement. In his first few weeks in the job, we'd been constantly at each other's throat. It was only after our so-called 'date', the result of a raffle which Kathy had rigged, that we'd buried the hatchet. It was during that 'date', that I'd discovered the reason for his mistrust of P.I.s. He'd been the lead detective on a kidnap case where the hostage had been killed, due in part at least to the negligence of the family's P.I.
Since our 'date', our working relationship had improved dramatically. How long that would last was anyone's guess.

Chapter 3

On my way to meet Maxwell, I passed Grandma's yarn shop—Ever A Wool Moment. As well as being a level six witch—the highest skill level—she'd also proven herself to be an expert marketeer. Not a week went by that she didn't come up with a new promotion.

This week's was front and centre in the window. A giant jam jar, almost as tall as the window, was crammed full of balls of wool. The poster in the window read, *'Win a year's subscription to Everlasting Wool'*.

Everlasting Wool was another of Grandma's innovations. Think Spotify or Netflix, and apply it to wool. How did it work? I had no idea. I suspected magic was involved, but she denied it. The person who guessed closest to the actual number of balls of wool in the giant jam jar would win the subscription. To make the window display more interesting, Grandma had persuaded (threatened?) one of her shop assistants to get into the jar with the wool. The poor woman was shoulder deep in yarn with only her head protruding. According to the poster, the competition would run until closing time. Hopefully, the young woman wouldn't need the loo before then.

"Care to have a guess?" Grandma appeared in the doorway.

"I think I'll pass. I don't really have much need for the subscription."

"You could give it to Annabel."

That was a thought—Mrs V could certainly make the most of an Everlasting Wool subscription. "Okay, then. What do I do?"

"Come inside."

Like a fly into a spider's web.

Grandma gave me a pen and an entry form which I quickly completed. I had absolutely no idea how many balls of wool were in the jar, so I put down the first number that came into my head.

"That will be ten pounds." Grandma held out her hand.

"What? I thought it was free to enter."

"Didn't you read the small print?"

"I didn't see any."

"Here." She handed me a magnifying glass, and now I could see that what had looked like a few random dots on the bottom of the poster, actually read: '*Entry fee = £10 - no refunds*'.

Jack Maxwell was waiting for me outside the coffee shop. Since our 'date', we'd taken to meeting on neutral ground.

"Shall we sit over there?" He pointed to a small alcove.

"Are you sure you wouldn't prefer the bench seats? They look a little more padded."

He looked confused for a few moments, but then the penny dropped, and he managed a smile. Since the 'rigged-raffle date', we'd been out together twice more. The first time, he'd tried to make me look an idiot at the bowling alley—although that hadn't exactly worked out as he planned. The second time, I'd had my revenge at the ice rink where he'd spent most of the time on his backside, which is why I'd just offered him the padded seat. Neither of those outings had been what I'd call a date, although I'm sure Kathy and Mrs V would have said otherwise.

"I'm sorry about the skating thing," I said when he brought our coffees to the table.

"No you're not."

"No, I'm not." I laughed. "Just being polite."

"I don't have very long." He checked his watch.

"You really know how to make a girl feel wanted."

"Unlike you, I have work to do."

Cheek! "I'll have you know that I'm rushed off my feet." The mystery of the squashed cupcakes wasn't going to solve itself.

"What can I do for you?" He winced as the coffee burned his lips.

"I'm just keeping you posted as promised. I'm working on the murder at Tregar Court."

"The 'Lift of Death'?"

"Why are you using the Bugle's headline?"

"Sorry, I shouldn't, but it's what everyone has started calling it. Who's hired you?"

"A friend of the victim."

"Friend? A woman?"

"Yes. They were just good friends apparently."

"That's what they all say."

"When did you become so cynical?"

"I was born that way. Anyway, you know the drill. Don't get in our way."

"I'll do my best. Is there anything you can tell me?"

"You know better than that."

"What about the CCTV. Can I see it?"

"I don't see why not. The management company at Tregar uses a security firm, Gravesend Security, to monitor the CCTV in their apartments. I can ask them to let you take a look at it. Another pair of eyes on it can't do any harm. Goodness knows, I've watched it enough times, and there's nothing to see."

"Nothing? I thought he was murdered in the lift."

"He was. He'd been stabbed when the lift reached the ground floor. The concierge saw him fall to the ground when the lift doors opened. But there's no sign of him being stabbed on the CCTV."

"That doesn't make sense."

"Tell me about it." Maxwell gave up on the coffee, which was hotter than Hades. "I have to get going."

"Okay, thanks. Will you let Gravesend Security know I'll be over later today?"

He gave me a thumbs up as he headed to the door.

Pearl phoned while I was on my way back to the office.

"Don't forget it's the baking competition tonight."

I'd lost all track of the days. "Did Aunt Lucy decide to enter in the end?"

"Yeah, that's why I'm calling. I thought you'd want to be there to support her."

I did, but it had totally slipped my mind. "Okay, I'll try to make it, but there's something I have to do first."

"Do your best. I know she'd love you to be there. You should see the cake she's made. It'll win easily."

"Sounds great. Look, I have to run. Probably see you later."

Gravesend Security was on a new industrial park, two miles west of Washbridge. If their own security was anything to go by, they should provide a good service to their clients. I didn't think I was even going to get through the gates at first; Maxwell's call hadn't come through. I was on the verge of breaking open the spell book when the man in the control box confirmed authorisation had been received.

"We've already given the police a copy," Tony said. In his late twenties, he had long hair and a nose which had been broken at least once. "How come you need to watch it here?"

The real reason was that Maxwell wouldn't have wanted his people to know he had given me access.

"I was in the area, so it made sense to view it here."

It didn't, and Tony knew it, but he pulled the CCTV up on-screen anyway.

"That's the fourth floor," he said.

The illuminated panel on the left hand-side confirmed the floor number.

"What about the fifth? Doesn't anyone live on the top floor?"

"Yeah, but the lift didn't get called to the fifth. The first people to get on were on the fourth."

The black and white images came from a camera which must have been mounted inside the lift, above the doors. A middle-aged couple entered and stood facing the doors. It began its descent, stopping again on the third floor where a man, who I recognised from press photos as the victim, entered the lift. The man didn't appear to speak to, or even acknowledge the couple. He stood at the front, facing the doors.

It began to descend again — passing the second floor without stopping. On the first floor, a young woman entered the lift. She too, didn't speak to, or acknowledge the other occupants. Apparently, neighbourhood spirit was alive and well in Tregar Court.

Once on the ground floor, the occupants vacated the lift.

"Is that it? I didn't see anything happen."

"Just a second." Tony used the mouse to bring up another tape. "This is taken from the lobby."

This second camera was situated on the ground floor. After a few seconds, the lift doors opened, and the victim, his chest stained with blood, fell face-first to the ground. The other occupants stepped over him into the lobby. The older woman appeared to be screaming. The younger woman was on her phone.

Afterwards, I was escorted out of the building by one of the secretaries. I could see why Maxwell hadn't objected to my viewing the footage. There really was nothing to see. The other occupants of the lift had been standing right behind the victim who had died from stab wounds to the chest, and yet they had seen nothing. Nor had anything been picked up on CCTV. It made absolutely zero sense, unless he'd been stabbed before he got into the lift.

"You were lucky," the secretary said.

"How do you mean?"

"Tony's a bit of a creep. He used to have wandering hands; if you know what I mean?"

"Used to? Did he get a warning or something?"

"He got a girlfriend. Don't ask me how. Someone told me she's a real looker too. No accounting for taste."

I used magic to transport myself to Candlefield. I wanted to make sure I was there in plenty of time for the baking competition. Pearl had told me to meet them at their place, above Cuppy C. I had my own room there where I kept a selection of clothes.

"Aunt Lucy and Grandma are going to meet us at the civic hall," Amber said.

"Grandma? Is she coming? After all she said about Aunt Lucy's baking?"

"She heard there's a free bar."

"She conned me out of ten pounds for a stupid competition—" I began.

"You won!" Amber said. "I almost forgot. Grandma said we had to tell you that you won the subscription. I didn't even know you knitted."

"I don't. I won—really?"

"Yep."

I was making a habit of winning competitions. Maybe I should start to do the lottery. But then, Kathy had rigged the raffle, and I wouldn't have put it past Grandma to have done the same. But then why would she? It wasn't like she'd do me any favours.

The baking competition was being held in the Washbridge Civic Hall. A grand title for a building which had seen better days. Stone steps with more filler than actual stone led to the outer hall, which was a fancy name for the waiting area.

Grandma and Aunt Lucy were already there when we arrived.

"Where's the free drink?" Grandma said.

"Have patience, Mother." Aunt Lucy's sigh suggested it wasn't the first time Grandma had asked that question. "It will be in the main hall."

"When are they going to open the doors? A body could die of thirst out here."

Aunt Lucy sighed again.

"Where's your cake?" I asked.

"All of the competitors had to bring them earlier so they

could be put on display before the main crowds arrived."
"What's the competition like?" Amber asked her mother.
"I'm cautiously optimistic."
"The standard must be really low then, if you ask me,"
Grandma said, as she checked her watch again.
"No one did ask you," Aunt Lucy snapped.

The doors opened, and the crowd headed by Grandma,
surged through to the main hall. Aunt Lucy led us to the
section where the iced sponge cakes were to be judged
while Grandma disappeared in search of the free bar.
"Oh no!" Amber screamed.
"No!" Pearl turned to her mother.
Aunt Lucy stared at what was left of her creation. The
cake looked as if it had been hit with a mallet.
"Who would do that?" I said.
Aunt Lucy was so shocked, she couldn't speak.
"What are you all looking so miserable about?" Grandma
had what looked like a double whisky in her hand. "It
looks like you could all do with a drink."
"Look, Grandma." Amber pointed to the remains of the
cake.
"That monstrous looking thing is never going to win
anything." Grandma took a swig of whisky.
There were times when I could have gleefully strangled
that woman.
"We may as well go home." Aunt Lucy turned away.
"Hold your horses." Grandma downed the rest of the
whisky. "Don't you want to stay and find out if you've
won?"
Surely, no court in the land would convict me for
murdering her.

Aunt Lucy began to walk towards the exit. The twins and I looked at each other, uncertain what to do.

"It's a good thing I hid your cake this afternoon." Grandma stooped down, lifted the tablecloth, and pulled out a magnificent iced sponge cake.

"How?" Amber stood open-mouthed.

Aunt Lucy turned around, and her face lit up.

"You lot are way too trusting," Grandma said. "I know how these people operate, and what they are capable of doing, so I magicked up a look-alike and put it on display."

"Thanks Mum." Aunt Lucy gave Grandma a big hug.

I'd never heard Aunt Lucy call Grandma 'Mum' before, and I'd certainly never seen them embrace.

"Put me down, woman." Grandma pulled away. "Don't you want to know who did this?" She pointed a crooked finger at the mangled cake.

"How can we find out?"

"I spiced the replacement cake with a special potion. It should be very easy to spot the culprits."

Sure enough, the perps were easy to identify. Grandma assured us that their pig noses would revert back to normal within twenty four hours. I'm not sure I believed her.

Grandma was on her third double whisky when it was time for the winners to be announced. It was all very tense. There were several worthy contenders in the iced sponge cake category.

'Second place goes to Ruth Landown. And the winner of this year's iced sponge cake category is Lucy – '

At that, the place erupted with cheers. Aunt Lucy was a

popular winner with everyone except the pig noses. The prize was a modest silver cup, but Aunt Lucy could not have been happier.

"Let's go home and celebrate," she said.

"Jill, you have to come with us," Pearl said.

I'd intended going back to Washbridge as soon as the winner had been announced, but I could hardly refuse to join in Aunt Lucy's celebrations.

"Will there be drinks?" Grandma hiccupped.

Chapter 4

A few of Aunt Lucy's closest friends joined us back at her house. There was hardly room to swing Winky.

"Where's Lester?" I asked the twins after we'd sneaked out into the garden.

"That's a good question," Pearl said. "He should have been here for Mum's big day."

"I'm not sure Mum knows where he is." Amber shivered — the night air was cold. "When I asked her about him, she fobbed me off."

"Do you think they've had some kind of bust up?" I glanced at the door to make sure no one had followed us outside.

"Who knows?" Pearl drank the last of her wine. "Old people are weird. I'm never growing old."

"Me neither," Amber said.

"Talking of old people." I hesitated long enough to check the coast was clear. "What's with Grandma? She spends all day criticising your Mum's baking, but then comes to the rescue like that."

"Typical Grandma. She loves to wrong-foot you. The moment you think you have a handle on her, she surprises you."

"Where is she anyway? I haven't seen her for a while."

The twins giggled.

"What?"

"We couldn't possibly tell you." They giggled again.

"Come on you two. What's going on?"

"You mustn't tell," Amber said.

"She'll kill us if she ever finds out."

Suddenly, I wasn't so sure I wanted to know.

"Come with us." Amber led the way back inside.

The main party was in the kitchen and dining room where the drink was still flowing, and music still playing.

Amber pointed to the door of the living room. "She's in here," she whispered.

Pearl put a finger to her lips. I nodded my understanding, but was beginning to regret ever asking about Grandma.

Amber opened the door as slowly and quietly as she could. What sounded like Wool TV was playing on the television. Amber peered inside, and then beckoned us to follow her.

The twins had their hands clamped tight over their mouths to stifle any laughter. When I saw the source of their amusement, I was too stunned to laugh or say anything. Grandma was on the sofa. She'd obviously fallen asleep, and had slumped to one side so her head was on the armrest. The side of her face was covered in jam and cream from the cake which was on a plate on the armrest.

I was terrified she might wake up, so led the way back out, through the kitchen and into the garden. The moment we were outside, the three of us dissolved into hysterics.

"We should have taken a photo." Amber was crying with laughter.

"Too dangerous." Pearl could barely speak. "She must never know."

"That we saw her?" I tried to catch my breath. "She can hardly punish us for that."

"Yes, well—" Amber glanced at Pearl.

"What?" I was getting a bad vibe.

"We didn't *just* see her."

"What do you mean?"

The twins giggled.

"What did you two do?"

"Well—" Pearl teased.

"Tell me!"

"We *might* have noticed that Grandma had fallen asleep," Amber said. "And we *might* have noticed that she was beginning to slump to one side."

"And we *might* have *accidentally* put a piece of cake on the armrest." Pearl laughed.

They both laughed. I didn't.

"You two are dead women walking."

"You were with us."

"I didn't put the cake on the sofa."

"I'm sure Grandma will believe you."

They were right. Grandma was more likely to think *I'd* done it than the twins. We'd had a few run-ins lately.

"You two are evil."

"Come on. You have to admit it's funny."

There was no denying that, but we were dealing with someone who wouldn't think twice about turning all three of us into dung beetles.

"I'm going to call it a night," I said.

"Aren't you going to stay around until Grandma wakes up?"

"No, because I don't have a death wish."

"Are you going back to Washbridge?"

"I thought I'd stay here tonight. I promised Barry I'd take him to the park in the morning."

"We're going to hang on here."

"Don't you two dare blame me for the cake."

"As if."

Their innocent expressions didn't fool me for a moment. If

Grandma had them in her sights, they'd throw me under the bus without a moment's hesitation.

I slept in my room above Cuppy C. Or at least, I tried to. What little sleep I did manage was filled with nightmares about giant jam and cream cakes, and dung beetles. I woke a little after eight o'clock. It came as something of a relief to find I still had only the two legs, and no overwhelming desire to roll balls of dung around the bedroom. I could hear no sign of life from the twins' bedrooms which meant that they were either still asleep or had been turned into scarabs too small to be heard.

"Let's go to the park," Barry said. "Can we? Please. Can we?"

Barry was my Labradoodle. His tail was wagging so vigorously it threatened to lift him off the ground.

What I wouldn't have given for some of his energy. It was taking all of my strength just to keep my eyelids open.

"Come on then, boy. The park it is."

"Yes! I love the park!"

He did too. Now that I'd had him for a while, I was a little more relaxed about letting him off the lead. He would run away and disappear for short periods, but he'd always come back in the end—at least that's what I'd thought.

"Barry?" It was over ten minutes since I'd last caught sight of him. The park was huge with numerous copses. "Barry!"

My phone rang. It was the call I'd been dreading.

"Jill? I've been trying to catch you for days," Drake said.

"Sorry, I've been kind of busy."

"Where are you?"

I thought about lying—saying I was in Washbridge, but

Drake lived close by, and for all I knew might have already seen me. "I'm in the park."

"Would you like some company?"

"Not right now. I have to get back to Washbridge soon."

"Oh. Okay. What about later in the week? I could come to Washbridge."

"I've got a lot on my plate at the moment. Sorry."

"Oh." I could hear the disappointment in his voice. "Okay then. Give me a call when things slow down."

"Sure. Bye then."

I hoped that might be the end of it, but something told me that Drake wasn't the type to give up so easily.

"Barry! Barry! Where are you?"

A couple: a witch and a werewolf were walking towards me. Their well behaved Westie was following a few yards behind them. Why didn't Barry do that?

"Hi, sorry to trouble you. Have you by any chance seen a black and white Labradoodle anywhere? I seem to have lost him."

The woman smiled. "He's more black than black and white now." She pointed off into the distance. "See those trees, close to the wall?"

It was a part of the park I'd never been in before.

"He's down there. In the swamp."

"The swamp?"

"It's not really a swamp. That's just what the locals call it. It's a shallow pond really. It's mighty muddy down there." She looked at my trainers, and gave me a sympathetic smile.

"Barry! No! Don't!"

Too late. He jumped up and planted his muddy paws

onto my clean, white t-shirt.

"Don't!"

Too late again. He shook himself from head to tail, covering me in water, mud and goodness knows what else.

Fantastic!

It wasn't just that he was wet and dirty. He smelled—real bad. Something must have fallen into the 'swamp' and died. There was no way I could take him home like that.

"That was fun!" he shouted, as I put on his lead. "Can I do it again?"

The dog groomers, Woof Wash, were only a stone's throw from the park. From outside, I managed to catch the eye of the woman behind the counter, and beckoned her to come out.

"Looks like he's been in the swamp," she said, when she saw Barry.

"How did you know?"

"We get a lot of our business that way."

"Is there any chance you could fit him in?"

"Yeah, no problem. We only have a couple of dogs booked in this morning. I'll probably need to give him a trim as well as a wash. Is that okay?"

"Sure. What time can I collect him?"

"He should be ready about one o'clock." She took his lead. "Are you sure you don't want to book yourself in too?"

I somehow managed to force a smile.

"What happened to you?" Pearl said.

"Barry and the swamp happened to me."

"You shouldn't have let him go in the swamp."

"Thanks for the tip. Where's Amber? Rolling dung around?"

"What?"

"Never mind. What happened when Grandma woke up?"

"Nothing. It's weird. When she came into the kitchen, she'd already wiped her face clean. She didn't say a word about it."

"That's scary."

"She must know it was us," Pearl said.

"Us? Hey, there's no 'us' about it. I wasn't the one who put the cake on the armrest."

"Maybe she'll let it go."

And maybe I'll win the lottery. "I'm going to get showered and changed."

"Good idea. You do kind of reek." Pearl pinched her nose.

After my shower, I felt much better. The clothes I'd taken off were beyond salvation, so I dumped them in the bin. I was still thinking about the conversation I'd had with Drake. He'd sounded disappointed and a little surprised. But then, so had I when Daze had told me about his past. Perhaps if he'd come clean right from the start, things would have been different.

With time to kill until I picked up Barry from the groomers, I volunteered to help out in Cuppy C. The twins were remarkably chipper, and both still had the giggles over the previous night's events. I wasn't so sure that it was over yet. Grandma wasn't the kind of person to let something like that go. I just hoped that I didn't get dragged into whatever punishment she decided to inflict on them.

"Are you looking forward to the school reunion?" I was

behind the cake counter with Amber. Pearl was busy in the tea room.

"I can't wait."

"Have you seen many of the people you were at school with since you left?"

"Yeah. Most of them still live around here—a lot of them are still with their parents." She glanced over at the tea room. "Can you keep a secret?"

"Sure."

"You mustn't tell Pearl. Promise?"

"I promise."

"At school, there was this one guy I used to have a crush on: Miles Best. He was hot with a capital 'O'."

Huh?

"I think he fancied me too, but he was a bit shy back then."

"What about William?"

"What about him? Nothing's going to happen. I'm just looking forward to seeing Miles again. That's all. You won't say anything will you?"

"Of course not."

As we approached lunch time, the tea room was getting busier. Pearl asked if I could help her out for an hour or so until it was time for me to collect Barry.

I took the orders and payments while Pearl and one of the other assistants made the drinks.

"You should see the dress I've bought for the reunion!" Pearl said, during a lull. "I look hot—even if I do say so myself."

"Hot with a capital 'O'?"

"Huh?"

"Never mind."

Pearl sneaked a glance at the cake shop counter to make sure Amber wasn't listening. "There's this guy I used to fancy at school. I can't wait to see him again."

"What about Alan?"

"It's only flirting. Nothing serious. Alan doesn't have to know. You won't tell him, will you?"

"No. Of course not."

"Or Amber? Promise?"

"I promise."

"He was the hottest guy in our year, and I'm sure he used to fancy me, but he was shy back then."

Oh dear. It couldn't be, could it? "What was his name?"

"Miles. Miles Best."

This wasn't going to end well.

Chapter 5

Barry had never looked cleaner. Or thinner. Or more cheesed off.

"I'm cold," he said, as I waited to pay.

"You'll be fine."

"They cut off all of my hair."

"Not all of it. Look." I ran my hand through his lovely, clean coat.

"I'll catch my death. Can I have one of those?" He looked across at the display of dog coats.

"Really? It's not that cold."

He shivered. I was sure he'd only done it for effect, but what the heck?

"What colour would you like?"

He gave me a look.

"Oh, yeah. I forgot. You can only see in black and white can't you?"

"Maybe, but I can see at least fifty shades of grey."

Everyone's a comedian.

"I like the one with the bones on it," he said.

Barry had a swagger to his walk on the way back home. Every time we passed by another dog, he gave them a *'check me out in my new bone-covered coat'* look. I had to admit, it did suit him. It had been an expensive morning what with the cost of the grooming, and the new dog coat. Time to get back to Washbridge to earn some money.

I popped into Cuppy C to let Amber and Pearl know I was leaving. They were still remarkably dung-free, so maybe Grandma had let this one slide.

Or maybe not.

"This is my sister," Mrs V said.

The woman seated next to her desk was a slightly younger version of Mrs V.

"Pleased to meet you." I offered my hand.

"So you're the private investigator. Annabel has told me so much about you." Mrs G had a surprisingly firm grip for a woman so petite. "Rather an unsuitable job for a woman, I would have thought."

Mrs V rolled her eyes.

"I manage," I said.

"I'm sure you do, dear." Mrs G released her grip, took out a handkerchief and wiped her hand. "I suppose it will have to do until the right man comes along."

"Have you seen your sister's trophy?" I said, ignoring her not so subtle dig.

"Yes, it's very—" She searched for the right word. "Big. It's a shame it's only a *regional* award. I've won so many of those that I don't bother to display the regional cups any more. I only keep the *national* trophies on display." She turned to her sister. "I forget, how many do I have now, Annabel?"

"You have five of them, G."

It was my turn to roll my eyes. No wonder Mrs V had an inferiority complex if this is how her sister had treated her over the years.

"I understand your grandmother has opened a new knitting shop," Mrs G said.

"She has. You should pay it a visit."

Mrs G and Grandma would get on like a house on fire.

"What a good idea. Come on Annabel, you can show me the Everlasting Wool which you were telling me about."

"I can't go now, I'm working—"

"Nonsense. Jill doesn't mind, do you dear?"

Mrs V looked at me with desperate eyes.

"Not at all. Don't rush back. Get lunch if you like."

How could I have been so cruel? Maybe Grandma's evil ways had begun to rub off on me.

"Where are those two bookends going?" Winky asked. He'd somehow acquired a dart board which he'd managed to set up on the wall above the leather sofa.

"Mrs V is taking her sister to the wool shop."

"Hopefully they'll stay there. One old bag lady is bad enough, but stereo ugly is too much for anyone to bear."

"Hey, be careful with those."

One of the darts had bounced out of the board and fallen onto the sofa.

"Don't get your knickers in a twist. Do you want a game?"

"I have work to do."

"I'll play you for a tenner."

"Where did you get ten pounds from?"

"Never mind that. Do you want to play or not?"

It would be the easiest ten pounds I'd ever made. He'd yet to get a dart in the board.

"One game."

"Yeah—ten pounds for the winner." Winky slapped a ten pound note on the sofa. "Now, let's see the colour of your money."

"Don't you trust me?"

"No."

Charming. I was the one who fed him, provided him with a home, and generally doted on him, but he didn't think I was good for ten pounds. "Here!" I slammed my tenner on top of his.

"You can go first." He handed me the darts.

I'd played occasionally at the local pub and, although I do say so myself, I was pretty good. I was certainly good enough to beat a one-eyed cat. Some might ask if it was ethical to take advantage of an ocularly challenged feline. To them, I'd say — *'Damn straight!'*

I got off to a good start with a dart in the twenty. My second dart slipped into the single five, but I pulled it back with a fantastic treble twenty on my last dart.

"Look at them babies!" I said, as I collected my darts.

Winky was all concentration. I probably should have gone a little easier on him. There was no need to rub his little face in it.

Treble twenty, treble twenty and another treble twenty.

"One hundred and eighty!" Winky shouted.

"You're a cheat!" I'd been hustled by a one-eyed cat.

He held up his paws — trying to look *'oh so innocent'*, but I was onto his game. The wayward darts he'd thrown when I walked into the room had been deliberate. He'd set me up, and I'd fallen for it: hook, line and tenner.

My confidence now gone, I managed only thirty five with the next three darts. Winky hit one hundred and forty, and had the gall to look disappointed.

Ten minutes later, with me back on two hundred and thirty, Winky wanted double-top to win. As if I wasn't already feeling bad enough, he turned around so his back was to the board, and then threw the dart over his shoulder. It landed smack bang in the centre of double twenty.

"I win, I think." Winky scooped up the money.

"You cheating —" I launched my first dart at the board as hard as I could. "Little —" The second dart bounced off the wall. "Fur bag!"

"Sorry to disturb you."

The man's voice caught me mid-throw. I turned to face him—dart still in hand.

"Don't shoot, I surrender." He smiled, but I detected at least a hint of nerves.

"Sorry." I put the remaining dart on my desk. "I was just—" Just what? Playing darts with the cat? Being hustled by the cat? Going insane? "I was just tidying up."

"Right. Yes." He edged into the office. "There was no one out there, so I came through."

"How can I help you, Mr—?" It was high time that I had a handsome hunk for a client.

"Luther Stone."

Luther Stone—wow! A superhero name to go with superhero looks and body. This was one case I was going to enjoy.

"How can I help you, Mr Stone?"

"Please call me Luther."

Just try stopping me.

"I have an appointment," he said.

"You do?"

"Your secretary contacted me."

"She did?"

Had Mrs V decided I was such a hopeless case that she'd hired a male escort for me?

He handed me his card.

"You're the accountant?"

"That's right. The lady said your previous accountant had left the profession."

"An accountant—like with numbers and tax and stuff?"

"Usually, yes. If I've called at an inconvenient time, I can always call again later. Or another day."

"No!" I said way too enthusiastically. "Today is fine. Right now is fine. My previous accountant, Robert Roberts, left all my books — would you like to see them?"

"Robert Roberts?"

"Yes. Strange man. He's now a hipster, food critic apparently. The books are in the filing cabinet in the outer office. You could use the desk out there if you like." Or my knee — whichever you prefer.

I piled the books onto Mrs V's desk. "If there's anything you need. *Anything* at all. Just give me a shout." I was going for 'smouldering', but judging by the look of terror on Luther Stone's face, I'd actually managed psychopath.

Would he notice if I snapped a photo to send to Kathy? Probably best to leave it — I didn't want to risk scaring him off. That didn't stop me from calling her.

"Hot accountant? Impossible." Kathy laughed.

"I'm telling you. He's sitting in the outer office right now."

"Photo or he doesn't exist."

"I can't, he already thinks I'm a nutter."

"Surely not."

It was time to take my mind off Luther.

"How's Peter's new job?"

"It seems to be going really well. Pete says Colonel Briggs is the best boss he's ever had. Pete's helping to organise the garden party."

"What garden party?"

"The one you said you'd go to."

"First I've heard of it."

"You and your memory."

This was one of Kathy's favourite ploys. Making out I'd agreed to do something when I knew nothing about it. "I hate garden parties."

"You hate everything: the theatre, circuses, garden parties — what *do* you like?"

"Hot accountants and custard creams."

"Anyway, you have to go to the garden party. Colonel Briggs made a special point of asking Pete to invite you. You could bring Jack."

"I think I'd rather bring Luther—"

"Sorry?" Luther Stone said. He'd popped his head around my door without my noticing.

I could feel the colour rising in my cheeks. "I was just— this is my sister." I pointed to the phone. "I mean — this isn't my sister — this is a phone. I'm talking to my sister. On the phone."

"Jill!" Kathy shouted. "Are you still there?" I pressed the 'end call' button.

I smiled at Luther. "I was just telling her, my sister that is, that I had a new accountant. She likes me to keep her updated on accountancy related matters."

"Right. I see." He clearly didn't. Yet another name added to the long list of people who thought I was a sandwich short of a picnic. "I've had a quick look at the books."

"Already? That didn't take long."

"There isn't too much to see."

Rub it in, why don't you?

"How often did your previous accountant meet with you?"

"Once a month."

"That's really not necessary. For this level of business, once a quarter should be more than enough."

"Really?" Only four helpings of Luther a year?

"I think so."

"Business has begun to pick up though. And I've sort of got used to the monthly meetings."

"It's your decision, of course. I was just trying to save you a little money."

"I think we should stick to the monthly meetings for now."

"Very well. Monthly it is."

This is what it had come to. Apparently, the only way I could get a man was to pay him by the month.

"What happened?" Kathy asked when I eventually picked up her call. I was en route to get a cappuccino, and possibly — who was I kidding — definitely, a blueberry muffin.

"Sorry. The accountant needed my attention."

"Did he now?" She laughed. "Why don't you bring him to the garden party?"

"I'm not sure Luther Stone is a garden party kind of a guy. He looks more like an extreme sports kind of a guy."

"He's an accountant."

"Yeah, that is kind of weird, I guess."

That's when I spotted them.

"Got to go."

"Jill?" Kathy shouted.

I ended the call, and stared at the coffee shop window. The pretty, curly-haired, blonde sitting with Jack Maxwell had way too much smile going on for my liking. And why was Maxwell laughing so much? He never laughed like that when he was in my company, and I was funny.

Granted, not always intentionally, but funny nonetheless.

I entered the coffee shop via the side door. It was busy, so I managed to get served and find a seat without Maxwell or his blonde floozy seeing me. It was of course purely coincidence that I chose the booth directly behind them. I couldn't see them, but I could hear every word they said.

"Bondy's never looked back." The floozy laughed.

"Couldn't have happened to a nicer man."

"Did you hear about Jules?" The floozy asked.

Whoever she was, they'd obviously known each other for some time. An ex girlfriend? Someone he used to work with?

"Jill!" Mrs V said. "G said she'd seen you come in here."

Mrs V and Mrs G were standing next to my booth.

"Jill?" Jack Maxwell's voice came over the seat.

Busted!

I stood up. "Jack? I didn't see you there." Not even I would have believed me.

"Do you want to join us?" Maxwell said. "This is Susan."

The floozy stood up, handed me the least sincere smile I'd ever seen, and said, "Hi."

"Hi. Thanks, but I have to get back to the office." I turned to Mrs V. "Why don't you stay and have a drink with your sister. I'll see you later."

"Thanks *very* much." She scowled. "By the way, I forgot to mention, the new accountant is coming today."

"A meeting with your accountant?" Maxwell said, as I made my way to the door. "Some people get all the excitement."

The floozy laughed.

Chapter 6

I didn't go back to the office. Instead, I went to Kathy's.

"What's the deal with your phone today?" She greeted me at the door. "Every time I call you, I get cut off."

"Must be a problem with the network," I lied.

"Do you want coffee?"

"No thanks, I've just had one."

"Are you still mad about the garden party?"

"Nah. I'll take one for the colonel."

"Who are you going to bring? Jack or Luther?"

"I'll probably go by myself. Luther is way out of my league."

"What about Jack? I thought you and he were an item."

"Me and Jack Maxwell have never been an *item*. We're working better together since your illegal manipulation of the raffle, but that's all. Anyway, Jack seems to have got himself a floozy."

"Is that even a word?"

"I just saw them in the coffee shop. She's all curls and peroxide. Definitely a floozy."

"Who is she?"

"Who cares? Susan somebody."

"You met her?"

"Kind of. I just happened to be in the next booth to theirs when Mrs V came charging in—"

"OMG, you were spying on them and got busted."

"Firstly, I was not spying on them. Secondly, I did not get busted. And thirdly, who over the age of fifteen says 'OMG'?"

Kathy laughed. "You so got busted. I wish I could have seen your face. I bet it was so red you lit up the whole shop."

"I was just having a coffee."

"So, not eavesdropping then?"

"I didn't even realise they were there."

"Liar. Who do you think she is?"

"I don't care."

"His girlfriend?"

"Which part of 'I don't care' don't you understand?"

"The part where you're lying through your teeth."

Based on the snippets of conversation I'd heard before Mrs V and Mrs G had shown up, I'd come to the conclusion that the floozy must have been an ex work colleague. That still didn't explain why she was in Washbridge unless there was more to their relationship. Not that I cared either way. Not even a tiny bit.

"What are those?" I said.

Kathy followed my gaze. "That one is a kangadillo and this one is a camoose."

"You are sick."

"What's wrong with them? Lizzie likes to dream up new creatures."

"So did Dr Frankenstein."

"Don't you think he's cute?" She tried to hand me the kangadillo, but I waved it away.

"My beautiful beanies. How could you do this to them? After all the years of love I gave them."

"Get over it."

"You can be a real bitch sometimes."

"Of course I can. I'm your big sister. It's in my job description." She put her hand on mine. "You know I don't mean it though, don't you?"

"Yeah, I know."

"Good. Well stop bitching then."

We both laughed.

"Holy moly. What's that?" I pointed to the offending object.

"This?" She picked up the ugliest toy I'd ever seen. "This is Things."

"Things? What kind of a name is that? And what's it supposed to be?"

"It *was* a rabbit, although you'd never know it now. We bought it for Lizzie when she was two years old. It's always been one of her favourite toys."

"Why is it called *Things*?"

"It used to sing before the mechanism inside of it broke."

"A singing rabbit? I still don't get the name."

"It was actually called Rabbit Sings but Lizzie couldn't pronounce her 'S's back then so she used to call it Rabbit Things. That got shortened to Things and the name stuck."

"It looks like it's on its last legs."

"It is. I don't know what we'll do when it finally gives up the ghost. Lizzie loves it to bits."

The roads were busy as I drove home. I saw the cyclist in my wing mirror as he came down the inside of the lane of traffic. At the head of the queue a double-decker bus signalled to turn left. The lights changed, and everything seemed to happen in slow motion. One second the cyclist was there, and the next he'd gone. A woman on the pavement screamed. The bus came to an abrupt halt. Two men in yellow hard hats who had been working on a nearby building, rushed over to the bus. I might have stayed put and waited for the traffic to start moving had it not been for the blood curdling scream which sent a shiver down my spine.

The traffic wasn't going anywhere, so I had no qualms about leaving my car. A small crowd of people had gathered around the front axle of the bus. The screams grew louder and more desperate. When I was some ten yards away, I saw him — the cyclist was trapped under the front wheel of the bus. His helmet was still on his head, and I could see no obvious head wounds. His face was contorted in agony, as he screamed again.

"The ambulance is on its way," someone said.

"We're going to need the fire brigade."

"They're on their way too."

But how would they ever get through? The gridlock now stretched in all directions as far as the eye could see.

"We have to get him out," a desperate voice said.

"How?" someone else said.

"We have to lift it," I said, as I stepped up to the side of the bus.

"One of the men in hard hats turned to me. "How are we meant to do that?"

"We have to try. Get as many people on it as you can."

He looked far from convinced, but he encouraged all the bystanders to take a hold of the bus. "On three," he said.

"One, two, three!"

I cast the 'power' spell, and the bus felt no heavier than a toy.

"Get him out!" hard hat guy shouted.

"Be careful," someone warned.

A man, and a woman who had identified herself as a nurse, pulled the cyclist from under the bus. The screaming had stopped, but only because he'd lost consciousness — probably a blessing.

"Down!" hard hat man said, and we allowed the bus to drop.

We congratulated one another, and in the distance I could hear the sirens.

The flash from a camera blinded me.

"Bugle." A scruffy man with a red nose shouted in my face.

Great. That was all I needed.

The next morning I was on my way out of the flat when my phone rang.

"Auntie Jill!" Mikey screamed. "You're a hero."

"What?"

"You're on the front page of the paper."

"I am?"

"Give me the phone, Mikey." I heard Kathy's voice.

"Morning sis. Have you seen the paper?"

"Not yet."

"Heroes lift bus." Kathy read the headline." There's a photo of you and the others."

"Does it say how the cyclist is doing?"

"According to the article, he's in intensive care but his injuries are not life threatening. The doctor said that if he'd stayed trapped under the bus any longer, things might have been much worse."

"Thank goodness he's alive. When I saw him under there, I thought he was a goner."

"How did you lift it? You're so puny."

"Gee thanks. It's not like I did it by myself. There were loads of us."

"According to an expert, it should have taken twice as many people as it did to lift the bus."
"Experts—what do they know?"

The photographs I'd seen of Tregar Court did not do it justice. The building itself, although relatively small—just five stories high—was hugely impressive. It was one of five executive apartment blocks in the Primetime Development, which was located in central Washbridge—just five minutes walk from my office.

The concierge, who was located on the ground floor, was ultra friendly. He said I was free to visit each apartment, but if the residents didn't want to speak to me, then I shouldn't push it. I wanted to take a good look at the lift, so decided to start at the top of the building—on the fifth floor. The lift was actually smaller than it had appeared on the CCTV. The lift opened onto a corridor. The only doors off the corridor were to the fire escape and the single apartment on that floor.

I rang the bell.

Susan Tagg was in her mid twenties, and a sports fanatic—her words, not mine. Not that I doubted her. You didn't get a body as toned as hers by sitting on the sofa eating chocolate—trust me I'd tried that approach.

"I never use the lift," she said.

"Never? What about when you're shopping?"

"I do my grocery shop online. It's delivered to my door."

Sounded like a great idea. I should really look into that.

"So you didn't use the lift on the day of the murder?"

She shook her head. "I'd left almost an hour before. I cycle to work."

Of course she did. "What do you do?"

"I work in the city. I'm a broker."

No wonder she could afford this place.

"Did you hear or see anything suspicious?"

"Like I told the police, I didn't see anyone that morning except the concierge. There aren't many people around at that time."

"How well did you know the victim?"

"Hardly at all. I don't really know any of the other residents. I say 'hello' if I see them in the lobby, but that's about it. I prefer not to get too friendly with neighbours."

I gave her my card in case she remembered anything else, but I wasn't optimistic.

I took the lift to the floor below where a married couple, by the name of Dixon lived. Mrs Dixon answered the door. I hadn't been sure what kind of reception I'd get—not everyone was willing to talk to a private investigator—but she couldn't have been more welcoming. After taking me through to the huge living room, and introducing me to her husband, she insisted on making tea for us all.

"Do you have any theories?" Mr Dixon asked, after settling down on a white leather sofa opposite the matching armchair I was seated in.

"Not yet, but then I've only just taken the case. Do you have any thoughts on who might have done it?"

"I wish I did. It's unnerving, as you can imagine. One minute the poor man was standing right in front of us, and the next he's lying dead in a pool of blood."

"And you didn't see anything?"

"Nothing. Have you watched the CCTV?"

I nodded.

"Damnedest thing. Wouldn't have believed it possible if it

hadn't happened right in front of me."

Mrs Dixon reappeared carrying a silver tray on which were china tea cups. Not a good idea when I was around.

"Biscuit?" The biscuit tin probably cost more than my car. I glanced inside. I guess money can't buy biscuit etiquette. Custard creams, digestives and ginger nuts—so very wrong.

"Not for me." I smiled. "Did you know the victim?"

"No. We tend to keep ourselves to ourselves. Everyone here does."

Thirty minutes later, and I hadn't learned much of anything except that tea didn't taste the same out of a china cup. Give me a good old fashioned mug any day.

There was no answer on the first or second floors. The victim had lived on the third floor.

"Any luck?" the concierge asked.

"There's nobody in on one or two."

"They're probably out together."

"Oh?" I sensed juicy gossip.

The concierge checked left and right in case anyone was within earshot. "The young man on two and the young woman on one seem to have hit it off, if you know what I mean?" He gave me a knowing wink.

"Are both of them single?"

"As far as I know. She seems to spend more time in his place than her own. You didn't hear that from me though."

"Mum's the word. I'll call back another day to see if I can catch them in. Thanks."

One thing I'd come to realise in this job is that there are two kinds of people in the world: those who refuse to tell you anything, and those who just love to gossip. Luckily for me, the concierge was the latter.

I'd planned an evening of spell practice because I wanted to be absolutely certain I had this week's spell mastered ahead of our next lesson. I didn't want to give Grandma any reason to pick on me.

As I walked from my car to the flat, I kept an eye open for Mr Ivers. After the speed dating debacle, he'd reverted to his boring self. Signing up for his movie newsletter had been a mistake of epic proportion. He now believed I was interested in his film reviews, and he missed no opportunity to waylay me whenever I had the misfortune to bump into him. Not tonight though—I was determined.

"Hello." The female voice took me by surprise.

"Oh, hello?" I said to the tiny, mouse of a woman who looked to be in her early thirties.

"I'm Betty. Betty Longbottom."

Great name. "Jill Gooder."

"I've just moved in down the corridor."

"Right. Just you?"

"Yes. I've been living with my parents."

Of course you have. "Do you work around here?"

"At the tax office. I'm a tax inspector."

Of course you are.

"Boring I know," she said.

"I suppose it has its moments."

"Not really, but then I do have hobbies."

Please don't tell me about them. Please don't tell—"

"I collect shells. Sea shells not gun shells." She laughed at her well worn joke.

The best I could manage was a polite smile.

"I bought cakes." She held out a large white box. "Would you like one?"

"That's very kind." I lifted the lid. It wasn't a difficult decision — the chocolate one was mine. "Thanks."

"Have you been to flat seven yet?" I asked.

"No, not yet."

"Make sure you do. Mr Ivers lives there. He's a very nice man."

"Okay. Thanks. I'll see you around."

"Bye, Betty."

If ever there was a match made in heaven.

Chapter 7

The white smock was a size too big, and the hairnet did nothing for me. How on earth did anyone work these hours? I'd started at Christy's Bakery at eight pm and wouldn't be finished until four am. It just wasn't natural. I was fighting a losing battle with my eyelids. My cover story was that I was a temp employed on the cleaning crew which comprised of me, Jimmy, an enthusiastic teenager, and Alison, the supervisor. Our job was to make sure that the floor was kept scrupulously clean at all times. Jimmy and I covered separate areas of the factory floor while Alison drifted from one to the other, making sure we were doing our jobs properly.

"You missed that corner," she said, over the noise of the conveyor belt.

"Sorry." I swept up the two offending crumbs. And I thought that *I* was a stickler for cleanliness. I should have taken Alison to Kathy's house—it would have blown her mind.

By break time, my back was aching. I wasn't sure I'd get through another four hours. Surely there had to be a spell I could use?

Everyone had brought their own sandwiches—everyone except me. I'd assumed there'd be somewhere I could buy a hot meal, but I'd been wrong. I had to make do with a packet of crisps and a bar of chocolate from the vending machine.

"Worked here long?" I said. I'd deliberately picked a seat next to Gary, the man who was responsible for loading the delivery vans.

"Too long." Gary was a werewolf; a very bored werewolf.

He seemed more interested in his magazine: Handbell Monthly, than in talking to me, but I persisted.

"So, you like bells?"

He gave me a look.

"Ringing them, I mean."

"I'm in a choir."

"You sing too?"

"A handbell choir."

"Right." Having exhausted my extensive knowledge of handbells, I tried to steer the conversation, such as it was, onto the subject of cake deliveries.

"Do you load all of the vans?"

He sighed, and put down the magazine. "Since they got rid of Eddie, yeah."

"Eddie?"

"Eddie Lingard. He and I worked together for six years. Good lad, Eddie was."

"What happened to him?"

"You'd have to ask the boss."

"Aren't they going to replace him?"

"Doesn't look like it. Why would they, when muggins here can do all the work? They still expect me to have all the vans loaded by four am."

Before I could ask another question, Gary had picked up his magazine and buried his head in it.

I could take a hint.

The shift ended, and Gary was out of the door on the stroke of four. I hung back a while because I wanted to speak to the drivers who I knew started at four thirty.

The first one to arrive, just after four fifteen, was Pauline, a witch with green and grey streaked hair. The grey was natural; the green, probably not. I remembered that Amber had mentioned that Pauline was the regular driver for the Cuppy C deliveries.

"Hi," I said.

"You made me jump. I didn't see you there."

"Sorry. I'm temping on the cleaning crew."

"Poor you. That job can be hard on the back."

"You've done it?"

"Yeah. Some years ago, mind. It was my first job. I was a temp too, but they kept me on. I drive the vans now."

"Do you like it?"

"I love it. Best job I've ever had."

"Isn't it hard work having to carry the deliveries from the van to the shop?"

"Not as hard as being on the cleaning crew." She laughed.

"I'm hoping to get something permanent," I said. "But I guess you won't be giving up your job any time soon?"

"No chance—unless they finish me." She was suddenly more serious.

"Why would they do that?"

"There have been problems with the deliveries. Cakes getting squashed."

"And they think it's your fault?"

"No one has come right out and said as much, but there have been a lot of questions. It's not fair. I take care with every delivery I make."

"How do you think it's happened then?"

"I don't know. I'm not even sure it has happened."

"What do you mean?"

"I shouldn't say."

"Go on. I'm not going to tell anyone, am I?"

"It could be the people at the other end—in the shops—

that are doing it."

"Why would they?"

"I don't know. Maybe to get a refund or to get better prices. The only thing I do know is that it isn't me who's doing it."

The cakes were packed into boxes by a team of four women. There was no way the damage could have been done at that stage because the four worked in such close proximity to one another. Once the cakes were in the boxes, they were passed to Gary who loaded them into the van. Then Pauline took over. That made Gary and Pauline the prime suspects, although having spoken to them, neither seemed to fit the bill. I had picked up one piece of potentially useful information though. Eddie Lingard, who used to work in dispatch, had been dismissed recently. A disgruntled ex-employee might want to get 'payback'. I'd have to find out from Beryl Christy why she'd got rid of him.

It was time to clock off. I headed back to my room at Cuppy C for a long warm bath, and some much needed sleep.

Aunt Lucy had invited me to her house for dinner—I'd assumed the twins would be there too, but I was wrong.

"How was your day at Christy's?" She scooped another spoonful of mashed potatoes onto my plate. Aunt Lucy's mash was to die for.

"Very tiring. I didn't wake up until mid afternoon." I yawned. "Where are the twins?"

"Working late. They're stocktaking." She laughed. "They'll probably be at it until midnight. They never were very good at maths."

"What about Lester? I haven't seen him for a while."

"He's been busy. Did you find anything out at Christy's?"

'He's been busy'? What did that mean? It was obvious that Aunt Lucy didn't want to talk about Lester, so I let it go.

"I spoke to the dispatcher and the driver—neither of them seem likely candidates. Pauline, the driver, said she thought the damage might be being done at the shops."

"Why would the shop owners do that? It doesn't make any sense."

"I know. I think she was clutching at straws because she feels like everyone is blaming her."

"What do you think?"

"I only had a chance to speak to her for a short while, but she didn't strike me as the kind of person to do anything like that. There is an ex-employee who I'm going to try to speak to."

I ignored Aunt Lucy's protests, and insisted on helping with the washing up. It was the least I could do after she'd made dinner for the two of us. Afterwards, we talked for over an hour while she showed me lots of photos of her and my mother as children.

"You look as though you got on well together," I said.

"Don't let these photos fool you. We used to argue more than the twins do."

"Is that possible?"

"Trust me on that one."

"Kathy and me are pretty much the same, but we still love one another to bits. Speaking of the twins, I think I'll go over there and see how they're doing."

"Don't let them drag you into the stocktaking. You know

what they're like."

The lights were still blazing at Cuppy C. I let myself in the back way, and popped my head into the shop. As usual, the twins were squabbling.

"It's thirty seven," Amber said.

"Thirty eight. Are you blind?" Pearl sighed.

"There's three rows of ten and then another—oh yeah, thirty eight."

"Thank you."

"I can't help it. I'm too tired. I can't see straight any more."

"Hi!" I walked towards the counter. "How's it going?"

"It would be going a lot better if Amber could count."

"You can't talk," Amber growled. "At least I know there are twelve in a dozen."

"I was referring to a baker's dozen."

"Liar. You—"

"Is there anything I can do?" I said.

"Thanks, but we're done now. How did it go at Christy's?"

I ran through the details again with the twins.

"It must be the ex-employee," Pearl said.

"It definitely isn't us."

"Are you sure?" I said.

They both glared at me.

"Joking. I'm only joking. I'll talk to Beryl Christy and her ex-employee, and let you know what I find out."

The twins decided to call it a day.

"We'd better sit at the back of the shop," Pearl said. "If anyone sees us drinking coffee and eating cakes, they will assume that we're still open."

Amber made the coffee—she'd lost the coin toss—and then the three of us helped ourselves to cakes.

"There goes the stocktaking figures," Pearl laughed.

"You really should start to sell blueberry muffins." I'd had to settle for a chocolate one—such were the hardships I had to endure.

"There's a very good reason we don't," Amber said, handing out the coffees.

"What's that?"

"Because we know you'd eat them all."

That was so true.

"Not long until the reunion now," I said, through a mouthful of muffin.

"I can't wait." Amber gave me a wink.

"Me neither." Pearl also gave me a wink.

Neither could I. It was going to be so funny when they discovered they'd both had a crush on the same guy. I was seriously considering sneaking into the reunion—I wanted to be there to see their faces when it all came out.

"What's that?" I'd only just spotted that there was a new poster on the notice board where the school reunion flyer had been.

"It's the 'Levels Competition'."

I walked across to get a closer look. The poster was short on detail. Apparently the annual 'Levels Competition' was to be held in one week's time in the Spell-Range.

"What is it exactly?" I asked.

"Grandma hasn't told you?" Amber grinned.

"No, she hasn't mentioned it."

"Oh dear." Pearl's grin matched her sister's.

I was getting bad vibes again.

"Grandma has entered you for it."

"She's done what? What is it anyway?"

"It's a competition for witches on levels one to five. Witches on the same level compete against one another, and the winner from each level competes in the grand final. The winner of the grand final is fast-tracked to become a level six witch."

"So in theory, a level one witch could end up as a level six witch?"

"In theory, but it's never happened. The lowest level witch who has ever won the final was on level four. Usually it's a level five witch who wins."

"Oh well, it would have been nice if she'd bothered to tell me, but I guess we'll have a few laughs."

"We?" Amber said.

"There's no 'we'," Pearl said. "You're on your own."

"I'm not doing it by myself. You two have to enter as well."

"We can't. To enter, your name has to be put forward by a level six witch."

"Why didn't Grandma put all of our names forward?"

"She has never put our names forward. She says we'd show her up," Amber said.

"If you're not doing it, then I'm not."

"You have to. We want you to. Don't we, Pearl?"

"Yeah, you have to. You can totally win level two."

"How? I've only just moved up from level one."

"You're a natural. And besides, there's another reason you have to take part."

"What's that?"

"Grandma will *totally* kill you if you don't."

Compelling reason.

"I don't suppose it'll hurt. It might be a laugh."
"I wouldn't let Grandma hear you say that. She's taking it super serious."
"No pressure then?"

Chapter 8

Mrs V was not happy—*again*. I could tell by the way she was taking her frustration out on her knitting. The needles were moving so quickly it was a wonder there weren't sparks.

"Is your sister still giving you a hard time?" I said.

"G always gives me a hard time, I'm used to her."

"What's wrong then?"

"It's your grandmother."

"You haven't fallen out again, have you?" Mrs V and Grandma had had a love/hate relationship ever since Ever A Wool Moment opened.

"Not yet, but we're probably going to."

"What has she done now?"

"You know what she's like with her promotional ideas."

I nodded. Grandma might not be my favourite person in the world, but the woman knew marketing.

"G was bragging about her national wins—as per usual, and your Grandma suggested we go head-to-head. Clash of the Titans, she called it."

"How?"

"Speed knitting. Your grandmother wants us to sit in the window of her shop and knit for four hours solid. The one who produces the longest scarf in that time will be crowned 'Ever A Wool Moment Speed Knitting Champion'."

"Catchy title. Are you up for it?"

"It doesn't look like I have a choice. Your grandmother has already told a local charity they can hold a collection in front of the shop. If I back out now, it'll look mean spirited."

"Can you win?"

"I don't know. I've never entered a speed knitting competition before, but I expect G will win. She wins everything."

As promised, the friendly concierge had called to let me know the young man and woman from floors one and two were back in residence. I was just about to go over there to see them when I heard someone come into the outer office. I didn't have any appointments—maybe Luther had more questions? I lived in hope.

"There's a Detective Shay to see you," Mrs V said.

"Who's he?"

"*She* works with Detective Maxwell apparently."

The floozy. "Send her in."

Detective Shay looked as though she'd just done sucking on a lemon.

"Jill Gooder." I forced a smile.

"Detective Susan Shay."

I began to laugh, but then caught myself.

"Something funny?" Detective Shay didn't wait to be invited to take a seat.

"Sorry, no nothing. Susan, did you say?"

She nodded.

"Sue Shay, Sushi?" I grinned. "Sorry, I imagine you get that a lot."

"What?" She looked puzzled.

"Nothing. Sorry. What can I do for you today, Susan?"

"Detective Shay."

So, that's how you want to play it, eh? "How can I help, *Detective Shay*?"

"I'm working with Detective Maxwell."

"Yes, I noticed that you seemed to be hard at it the other day in the coffee shop."

"When you were hiding in the next booth?"

Touché. "I wasn't hiding, like I said to Jack —"

"It doesn't matter. I just want to get a few things straight."

She should have started with her hair. No one was going to take her seriously with those curls.

"I worked with Detective Maxwell for six years in Camberley."

Worked? Just worked?

"We made a great team until he requested a transfer."

"After the Camberley kidnap?"

"You know about that?"

I nodded.

"Then you'll understand why we don't need an amateur P.I. interfering in our work. Stick to the things you're good at: unfaithful partners, missing dogs."

Turning you into a toad? My natural instinct was to tell her where she could shove her blonde curls, but I didn't want to give her ammunition to use against me with Maxwell.

"I know what happened in Camberley," I said. "Jack and I have discussed it. I would never do anything which would endanger someone's life. Wherever possible, I'll keep him posted of —"

"From now on, you deal with me."

"Does that come from Jack?"

"No, it comes from me."

I'd had quite enough of Sushi. "If that's everything, I have an appointment."

She stood up. "What's that ugly thing?"

Winky had been fast asleep under my desk, and had only

now decided to see what all the noise was about.

"Winky isn't ugly. He just has eye issues."

"You should put some kind of warning on the door. If someone had a dicky heart—"

"Thank you for coming to see me today, Detective."

"Just remember what I said."

"Who does she think she's calling ugly?" Winky said, after she'd left. "Did you see her hair?"

I took the lift to the first floor. The papers had mentioned that Darcy James was a part time model. She didn't look much like one today, with her oversize curlers, jogging bottoms and green face pack.

"Who are you?" she said.

"My name is Jill Gooder." I flashed my card quickly in front of her face. "I'd like to ask you a few questions about the murder."

"I've already told your people everything I know."

Hey, if she thought I was the police, who was I to correct her?

"I just have a couple of questions. It won't take long."

"I suppose you'd better come in." She sighed, and took a seat on the sofa.

It's okay, I'll stand.

"You were in the lift when the murder took place?"

"Yeah, but I didn't see anything. Not until he dropped down dead."

"Did you know the victim?"

"I'd seen him around, but we'd never spoken."

"Not even a 'good morning'?"

"No."

Probably too busy checking her Facebook messages or

tweeting. She looked the sort—not that I was judging.

"What about the other residents? How well do you know them?"

She shrugged. "I don't speak to any of them."

"No one?"

"I just said, didn't I?"

Beauty, charm and a liar.

"I understand you're a model, Ms James?"

"Miss. I don't go in for all that 'Ms' rubbish. Only part time."

"What do you do the rest of the time?"

"I'm studying for a degree in psychology."

After I'd knocked for the third time, I was beginning to think the man on the second floor must have slipped out. Then the door opened.

"Hello?" He peered around the door which was on a chain.

"Morning. Jason Allan?"

He nodded but made no eye contact.

"I'm Jill Gooder. I'm investigating the murder in the lift, and I'd like to ask you a few questions."

"What kind of questions?"

"Just routine. It should only take a few minutes."

"I have to go out shortly."

"Like I said, it won't take long."

He slid off the chain, and opened the door. It wasn't a pretty sight.

"Sorry about the mess." He led the way inside. "I need to tidy."

He'd got that much right. The apartment looked like an explosion in a launderette. There were clothes, most of them dirty, all over the floor, and on every surface.

"Take a seat," he said.

Every chair was covered with clothes—including some unsavoury looking underwear.

"It's okay. I'll stand."

I ran through my usual list of questions. His answers were slow and ponderous. I wasn't sure if he was nervous or high on something.

"What do you do for a living?"

He shrugged. Maybe the question was too difficult. I rephrased it.

"Where do you work?"

"I don't have a job. Not at the moment anyway. I used to be a carpet fitter, but I had to give it up. Problems with my knees. The job's murder on the knees."

"I can imagine. Do you know any of the other residents?"

He shook his head.

"Are you sure? What about the woman on the first floor?"

His cheeks flushed red, and he began to shuffle around on the chair. "I don't know her."

"You're sure?"

"Positive."

I wasn't sorry to get out of his apartment. That made two for two in the dishonesty stakes. Darcy had denied she knew Jason—which to be honest, was understandable, and he'd denied he knew her. What did they have to hide? And, how were they paying the rent on this place? I hadn't checked the actual figures, but there wouldn't be much change out of two thousand pounds a month. Darcy's part-time modelling and Jason's carpet fitting, when he was actually working, wouldn't cover that kind of outlay.

I took the stairs, and bumped into the cleaner in between the first and second floors.

"Do you have a minute?" I said.

"Sure. Nothing exciting going on here."

"Were you working when the murder happened?"

"No. It was my day off. I work two on and one off."

"Do you clean the apartments?"

"No. Just the common areas. Some of the residents employ their own cleaners."

Not the guy on two obviously.

"Do you talk to the residents?"

She laughed. "Me? I doubt they know I exist. I'm invisible."

"I bet you see what goes on though."

"Maybe."

"Do you have any ideas about who might have committed the murder?"

She shook her head.

"Anything you can tell me? Did you witness any arguments between the residents?"

"No arguments, but—" She seemed unsure whether to continue.

"Go on. I won't mention this to anyone."

"I suppose you already know about those two? The woman on one and the man?"

I nodded. This was confirmation that the concierge had been correct about Darcy and Jason. So why had they denied knowing one another?

I called Jack Maxwell's number. I didn't have anything

much to report—it was more a courtesy call to let him know I'd spoken to all of the residents of Tregar Court.

"Detective Maxwell's phone."

I recognised Sushi's voice immediately.

"Is Jack there?" I said.

"Gooder, is that you?"

The last time someone had addressed me as Gooder was when I was at school.

"Yes. Can I speak to Jack, please?"

"I've told you. Your point of contact is me now. What do you want?"

Aside from dipping you head first into a vat of acid?

"Nothing, it isn't important. Will you tell him I called?"

I didn't wait for the reply—I already knew what it would be.

"Slow down! I can't understand what you're saying." Kathy grabbed me by the shoulders. "Take a deep breath."

I took several but it didn't help. I was ten degrees north of livid.

"She's a cow!" I said.

"Who is?"

"A poisonous cow!"

"Who are you going on about Jill?"

"Sushi!"

"Have you been inhaling yarn fumes again? You know how that affects you."

"Detective Susan Shay. Sushi."

"Has Jack Maxwell moved on already?"

"No. He's still here, but now he has a minder. Susan *Sushi* Shay. She had the bare-faced cheek to warn me off."

"Warn you off what?"

"Not what. *Who*. Jack Maxwell. She said she's my point of contact now. I'm to leave Jack alone."

"What does he say about it?"

"Nothing. I don't know. I can't get near enough to find out. He's too busy hiding behind his blonde floozy."

"Well," Kathy said. "It's a good thing you don't care about him otherwise you might really be upset."

She ducked just in time to avoid the kangadillo which I threw at her.

"I'm not upset. This isn't upset. This is angry!"

"So what are you going to do about it?"

"What can I do?"

"You have to get Maxwell on his own. Maybe he doesn't realise what his new partner is up to."

"How am I meant to get him on his own when I can't get near him?"

"Come on, Jill. You're the resourceful one."

Kathy was right. I did need to get Jack Maxwell on his own. If this really was the way he wanted things to be, then he should at least have the decency to tell me to my face.

Chapter 9

I didn't want to be seen talking to Beryl Christy in the bakery, so I'd arranged to visit her at home—a rather grand house on the east side of Candlefield. There must be money in baking—Aunt Lucy should set up her own business.

"Mrs Christy, thanks for seeing me."

"You really must call me Beryl. Come inside."

Tea and cakes were served on the decking at the rear of the house. The gardens were huge and well maintained.

"You have a lovely home."

"Thank you. My late husband and I bought it many years ago. It's really much too big for me now that I'm all alone, but I can't bring myself to move."

"I spent some time undercover in the bakery."

"How did it go?"

"Nothing much to report yet. There is one thing I wanted to ask you though. I understand you recently dismissed an employee from the dispatch department."

"Eddie Lingard. That's correct."

"Would you mind telling me why you sacked him?"

"I'm sorry but it's a personal issue. It has nothing to do with the damaged cakes; I can assure you of that. I can vouch for Eddie."

Now I was intrigued, but before I could press her further, a voice from inside the house interrupted us.

"Mum? Mum?"

Beryl Christy stood up and walked back towards the open French doors. "Annie, we're out here."

"I should have known you'd be out here." Annie gave her mother a hug.

"Annie, this is Jill Gooder. I told you about her."

"The private investigator." She held out her hand. "How exciting."

"Not really."

Annie had the firm grip of a confident woman.

"I'd better be going," I said.

"Don't let me drive you away if you still have things to discuss."

"It's okay. We were done anyway. Thanks again."

Why had Beryl Christy been so secretive about her dismissal of Eddie Lingard? Something smelled fishy.

"You two look gorgeous," I said.

The twins beamed back at me. I'd never seen them so excited. It was the night of the school reunion, and both Amber and Pearl were looking forward to seeing Miles Best. Little did they know that they both had their eyes on the same guy. He must have been something special to have aroused all of that passion.

I knew it was wrong, and I realised I shouldn't have done it, but I couldn't help myself. There weren't too many comedy gold moments like this, and I was determined to be there. I couldn't wait to see the twins' faces when they realised that they were both hoping to meet up with the same guy. I had my car with me, so I offered to give them a lift to the school. They were so excited they barely paused for breath all of the way there.

"Enjoy yourselves!" I called after them.

"We will!"

I parked at the far side of the car park, and waited until I thought everyone would be inside. The music coming from the large hall was loud enough to dance to in the car park. I sneaked up to one of the windows on the side of the building, and peered inside. The hall was packed — school reunions were obviously much more popular in Candlefield than they were in Washbridge. Wild horses couldn't have dragged me to mine.

I had planned to use magic to get inside, but the hall was so busy that I felt confident I'd be able to hide among the crowd without the twins spotting me. Where were they anyway? I needed to be sure before I went charging inside. It took me a few minutes, but I eventually spotted them next to the bar. There was no one standing with them, so they obviously hadn't spotted their prey yet.

"Hello?" The man's voice made me jump.

"Oh, hi."

"Are you okay?" he asked.

"Yes, I was just — err — looking to see how many people are here already."

"Do I know you?" He studied my face. "Were you in my year? I don't remember your name."

My mind went blank — I glanced around. "It's Lawn."

"Lawn?"

"No, Dawn."

"Dawn — ?"

"Dawn — err — Tree."

"Dawn Tree?"

"Yeah. I joined half way through the first year."

"Oh yeah. Dawn Tree. I remember you now. I'm Miles. Remember?"

"Miles Best?"

"I know. I've put on a few pounds."

A few? Way more than a few based upon how the twins had described him. "I barely noticed."

"And the hair," he said. "Gone!" He ran his hand across his bald head.

"It suits you."

"Thanks. I've been looking forward to tonight for ages."

"Me too."

"I used to be really shy at school," he said. "I was too scared to speak to any of the girls."

"Looks like you've come out of your shell."

"I sure have. There's no stopping me now."

"Is there anyone in particular you're looking forward to seeing?"

"Two people actually. You might remember them. Twins: Amber and Pearl."

"Didn't they have ginger hair?"

"That's them. Have you seen them?"

"I think you're in luck. They're standing by the bar."

"Fantastic! Shall we go in?"

"You go ahead. I—err—I left something in the car. I'll be right along."

"Okay." Miles Best headed for the entrance. "I'll see you inside."

The twins had their gazes fixed on the door. I had mine fixed on them. Both girls reacted when they saw the door open, but relaxed again when they saw the fat, bald guy walk in.

I glanced over at Miles. He'd spotted his quarry.

He strode across the dance floor—a man on a mission. The twins were still staring at the door—barely noticing his approach.

"Three, two, one—bingo!"

Miles was standing in front of them now. Their expressions changed from surprise to confusion to 'get me

out of here'.
Priceless! I headed back home.

It was just after midnight when I heard the footsteps on the stairs.
"Hi girls, how was it?"
Amber and Pearl shared the same dejected expression.
"It was okay." Amber managed half-heartedly.
"The music was too loud." Pearl kicked off her shoes.
"Did you see lots of old friends?"
"Some."
"A few."
"Anyone in particular?"
"Not really."
Amber disappeared into the bathroom.
"Did you see Miles?" I whispered to Pearl.
"No." She shook her head. "He wasn't there."
"Shame."
"I'm going to bed," she said.
"Did you see Miles?" I caught Amber on her way to her bedroom.
"He didn't turn up."
"Shame."

Back in Washbridge, I was so busy thinking about the twins and Miles Best that I almost collided with Betty Longbottom. "Oh, hello. How are you settling in?"
"Very well, thanks. Everyone seems very friendly."
Too friendly if you ask me. "Did you meet Mr Ivers?"
"No. I knocked on his door but there was no answer."
"You should try again. I'm sure you'll like him."
"Okay. I will."

"Bye, then." I made to leave, but Betty blocked my way.

"Jill? Is it okay if I call you Jill?"

"Sure."

"I was wondering if you were doing anything tonight?"

I didn't like the way this was going. Time for the 'forget' spell methinks.

Betty looked a little puzzled. "I've totally forgotten what I was going to say."

"Oh well, never mind. Look, sorry but I have to rush."

"Jill!" Mr Ivers appeared from nowhere. What had I done to deserve this?

"I have your newsletter!"

"Thank you." I tried to contain my excitement. "By the way, have you met our new neighbour? Betty, this is Mr Ivers. Mr Ivers, this is Betty Longbottom. Betty is a tax inspector."

"Pleased to meet you," he stuttered.

"Do you like cake?" Betty said.

"What kind? I'm allergic to coconut."

"Sorry," I interrupted. "I have to rush. Bye."

Just call me Cupid. That should get those two off my back for a while.

I almost dropped my spagbol when a voice from behind me said, "That looks tasty."

"Mum, you scared me to death."

"Death isn't as bad as they make it out to be. I'm having quite a hoot."

Even so, I wish you wouldn't creep up on me like that."

"Sorry, dear. I didn't mean to make you jump."

My birth mother died shortly after she'd told me I was a witch. Since then, her ghost had attached itself to me (technical term for haunting) and appeared at regular intervals. She'd recently married her childhood sweetheart, Alberto, another ghost. I'd been one of the bridesmaids—a nightmare in pink.

"How do you feel about the Levels Competition?" my mother said.

"It would have been nice if Grandma had bothered to ask me first."

"You know how she is."

"I'm beginning to."

"Still, it's quite a compliment. You're the first witch she's ever put forward."

"I feel bad for the twins."

"You shouldn't. I really don't think they're all that bothered, and they're certainly not good enough. They're more interested in Cuppy C. Oh, and while I remember, thank you for being a bridesmaid."

"That's okay, but I wish you'd told me before the day of the wedding."

"I was afraid you wouldn't show up."

She was probably right. "Of course I would have. I wouldn't have missed it for the world. How's Alberto?"

"Lazy. I'd forgotten just how lazy men can be. Take my advice, don't get married."

"You've only been married for five minutes."

"I'm only joking. I love him to bits really. I just need to get him trained. I was sorry to see you've ended things with that nice young man you came to the wedding with. What's his name? Drake?"

"Things just didn't work out."

"And you don't seem to be doing much better with your other young man—the detective."

"That never really was a thing."

"Guess I shouldn't hold my breath for grandchildren."

"I've given up on men." I hesitated. "Look—I—err—don't know how to say this."

"What is it?"

"I don't mean this to sound unkind, but—."

"Go on. Spit it out."

"It's just that I feel a little uncomfortable, knowing you're following me around all the time."

"I'm your mother."

"Which is precisely why I don't want you looking over my shoulder. No child wants their parents following them around."

"But I worry about you."

"I'm fine, honestly. You said yourself that I'm doing okay at this 'witch thing'."

"You are. You have the potential to be a great witch, but The Dark One is so dangerous."

"I need you to give me some space. If I'm in trouble, I'll call for you."

"I worry so much—"

"So does *every* mother. That goes with the territory."

"You're right. I know you're right."

"So, will you promise not to follow me around any more?"

"I promise to try my best, but a mother can't help worrying."

"Okay, thanks. While you're here, would you mind if I asked you something?"

"Of course, anything."

"I was just wondering about—well about ghosts."

"What exactly?"

"This probably sounds like a stupid question, but where do you live?"

"It's not a stupid question at all. We live in another plane or dimension."

"Really?"

"No, of course not." She laughed. "We actually live in a place known as GeeTee."

"GeeTee?"

"Short for ghost town."

I waited—fully expecting her to laugh again, but she didn't.

"Think of it like Candlefield. Humans don't know that Candlefield exists, and yet it is home to all the sups. GeeTee is much the same. Ghosts live there, but it is invisible to humans and sups alike."

"It's not really called GeeTee is it?"

"No, of course not. Its actual name is Grande Tramagne, hence the 'GT'. No one calls it that though. Everyone calls it Ghost Town or GeeTee."

"What's it like there?"

"Just like any other city except the only people who live there are ghosts."

"Are there houses and shops, and roads?"

"Yes, all of those."

"Are there human ghosts in GeeTee too or is it just sups?"

"Both. Sups lose their powers once they become ghosts, so everyone is pretty much the same."

"And the only way that the living can see a ghost is if the ghost attaches itself to the human?"

"More or less, although a powerful witch can extend that for a short period of time like Grandma did at my wedding. But generally, yes. Then of course there are the human psychics. A few humans are born with the power to see and communicate with ghosts, but they are few and far between. Most of the ones you hear about are charlatans."

"That must be pretty weird for them."

"I imagine the worst part is that no one will believe them. There are even rumours that a few exceptionally powerful psychics are able to move between the human world and GeeTee, but I'm not sure I believe that."

"Wow. It's hard to take it all in. If I think of any more questions, can I—? "

"Just give me a shout."

My phone rang.

"Gooder!"

It was my favourite curly, blonde detective.

"Hi, Sue."

"Detective Shay to you."

"What can I do for you, *Detective Shay*?"

"There have been complaints."

"Ignore them. You're doing a great job."

"Complaints about you. Residents of Tregar Court have reported that you've been harassing them."

"Which residents?"

"Never mind. You shouldn't have been there at all. Murder is police business. Stick to what you're good at. Isn't there a missing dog you could be tracking down?"

I took a deep breath, and somehow resisted the urge to let her know what I really thought of her. "I informed Jack that I'd be working on this case."

"How many times do I have to tell you? I'm your point of contact now. Is that clear?"

"Crystal."

"This is your last warning. Next time I won't be so understanding."

"Have a nice day, Detective Shay."

Who did she think she was, and why was Maxwell allowing her to talk to me like that?

Chapter 10

The day of the speed knitting event had arrived. As usual, Grandma had ramped up the marketing to fever pitch. The man-size balls of wool were once again freaking out the residents of Washbridge as they handed out their flyers. The Bugle had a small article on the front page, and there had been coverage on local radio as well as on Wool TV.

It was scheduled to start at ten am with the winner being announced just after two pm. I'd told Mrs V she needn't come into the office, but she was there bright and early as usual.

"Are you okay?" I asked, but I already knew the answer.

"I'll just be glad when it's all over."

"How is your sister?"

"Oh, G loves all the attention. She absolutely adores the limelight. She spent most of last night practising her autograph."

"You never know, you might win."

"Against G? Not a chance. She's beaten me at everything ever since we were kids. She'll get more satisfaction from beating me than she will from actually winning the event."

"How long is she staying for?"

"She's going home tonight, so at least I have that to look forward to." Mrs V sighed. "Will you come along and support me?"

Four hours in Ever A Wool Moment would feel like a lifetime. I had planned to give the place a wide berth until this fiasco was over, but how could I say no?

"Sure, I'll be there."

"Thanks, Jill. A few members of my club have promised to come too, but I have a feeling they'll be outnumbered by G's fans."

My phone rang. It was Aunt Lucy.
"Jill, I'm sorry to disturb you."
She didn't sound herself, and my first thought was that something had happened to Lester. "What's wrong?"
"Do you think you could come over? I wouldn't normally ask, but—"
"What is it? Is Lester all right?"
"Lester? He's fine. It's the twins."
"Are they okay?"
"Err—yes, they're not ill or anything like that. It's just—if you could come over it would be easier to show you than to explain over the phone."
"Okay. I'll come now."
"Go straight to Cuppy C. I'll meet you there."
I told Mrs V I'd been called away on an urgent case, but promised that I'd be back in time for the knitting competition.

I was getting much better at using magic to travel between the two worlds. My early attempts had been painful (I'd landed with a thud on my backside) and inaccurate (I'd never been able to predict exactly where I'd land). If Grandma had taught me anything, it was the importance of focus. Now, whenever I travelled between Washbridge and Candlefield, I made sure to concentrate on the exact location I wanted to reach.
The first thing I noticed when I arrived at Cuppy C was that neither of the twins was in the shop.

"Where are they?" I called to one of the harassed assistants.

She gestured that they were upstairs. Perhaps they were both ill and needed me to help out? Judging by the queues, someone would need to give the overworked assistants a hand.

Aunt Lucy was waiting for me at the top of the stairs.

"What's happened? Where are they?"

"Your *grandmother*. That's what's happened."

Aunt Lucy led the way into Amber's bedroom where both girls were sitting on the bed. Their faces were red and blotchy from crying. Neither of them had changed out of their pyjamas, and both of them were wearing knitted beanie hats.

"Amber? Pearl? What's happened?"

"I hate her!" Pearl screamed.

"How could she do it?" Amber began to cry.

"What? What has she done?"

"Show her," Aunt Lucy said to the girls.

"I can't." Pearl was crying now too.

"You have to. Show her."

The girls bowed their heads, and then slowly removed their hats.

"No! What?" I was too stunned to put together a coherent sentence.

The girls quickly pulled the hats back over their heads to hide the donkey's ears that had replaced their own.

"She's pure evil." Amber sobbed.

Aunt Lucy touched my shoulder and gestured for me to follow her. Once we were in my bedroom, she closed the door behind us.

"Why would she do something like that?" I said.

"Revenge. She knew it was the twins who'd put the cream cake on the sofa."

"Even so, this is a bit much isn't it? It was only a joke."

"Grandma doesn't do jokes—particularly if they're at her expense."

"How long will the spell last?"

Aunt Lucy shook her head. "That's just it. She says it will last for a year."

"That's ridiculous. Can't you reverse it?"

"I can't reverse a spell cast by a level six witch. The only person who can reverse it is Grandma or a more powerful witch."

"Is there one?"

"Not that I know of. There are other level six witches, and it's possible that there may be a more powerful one, but there's an unwritten code that they do not interfere with each other's spells."

"What are we going to do?"

"That's why I asked you to come over. I want you to try to persuade Grandma to reverse the spell."

"Me? She won't listen to me. She hates me."

"She most certainly doesn't hate you."

"She does an awfully good impression then."

"She respects you."

"She has a strange way of showing it."

"Will you try? Please."

"Of course. I just don't think—I'll try."

The girls must have been eavesdropping at the door.

"You have to make her reverse it," Amber said.

"Please, Jill." Pearl hugged her sister. "Tell her we promise never to do anything like that ever again."

"Yeah." Amber sobbed. "Tell her we'll be good."

Ever A Wool Moment was heaving with people. Mrs V and Mrs G were seated at separate tables in the window. Mrs G was all smiles—Mrs V, not so much. Grandma was also in the window, standing in between the two tables posing for the photographers who were lined up outside. I'd never seen so many paparazzi in one place—all this for a knitting competition!

Grandma raised a hand to silence the crowd. "We start in five, four, three, two, one. Go!"

The crowd erupted. There were dozens of voices urging on Mrs G, and just a few encouraging a very unhappy Mrs V.

"Can I have a word?" I'd managed to fight my way through the crowd to Grandma.

She gestured to the small store room at the back of the shop.

"It's a good crowd." She scratched her wart with a crooked finger. "Takings should be through the roof today."

"I'm not here to talk about your stupid shop." Whoops! Great opening move, Jill.

"I'm sorry? What did you just say?"

"Sorry. I didn't mean that. I'm just a little upset."

"Why's that? Love life still in the toilet?"

"Why would you do that to Amber and Pearl?"

"Is that all?" She cackled. "I thought it was something important."

"It is important. You've turned their—"

"I know what I did. I think their new ears suit them."

"Reverse the spell!"

Her smile melted away. "I'm sorry. What did you say?"

Oh boy. "I asked you to reverse the spell."

"It didn't sound like you were *asking*. It sounded like you were *telling* me what to do."

"I'm sorry. *Please* will you reverse the spell?"

"No. Those girls have to be taught a lesson. They should respect their elders and betters."

"What they did—it was just—a practical joke. Maybe they shouldn't have done it, but—"

"There's no *maybe* about it."

"Okay. They shouldn't have done it, but that doesn't mean they deserve to suffer like this. For a whole year?"

"I had thought of making it permanent. I must be getting soft in my old age."

"You have to reverse it."

"What have I told you? I don't *have* to do anything." She glared at me, and then the evil smile returned. "But, I'm a reasonable woman."

And I'm the Prime Minister.

"Tell you what I'll do," she said. "We'll have a wager on the speed knitting competition. If your horse wins—"

"Please don't refer to Mrs V as a horse."

"If Mrs V wins, then I'll reverse the spell. If she loses, then the spell stands. I can't be fairer than that."

Grandma knew exactly what she was doing. She knew she was backing the favourite.

"That doesn't work for me," I said.

"Oh well." She turned to leave.

"Reverse the spell or I won't take part in the Levels Competition."

If I thought I'd seen Grandma angry before, I'd been wrong.

"What did you say?"

Any moment now, she'd cast a spell on me, and it wouldn't be only my ears that were transformed.

"I said—" It was hard to concentrate with her wart so close to my face. "If you don't reverse the spell, I won't take part in the Levels Competition."

"What makes you think you have a choice? I can make sure you're there."

"But you can't force me to try. I'll throw it."

Grandma pointed her crooked finger in my face. Any moment now, she'd rip my eye out—and eat it probably.

"Six months." She spat the words.

"What?"

"I'll reduce the spell to six months."

"You have to reverse it *right now*."

"One week, and that's my final offer."

"Twenty four hours."

"Forty eight."

"Done."

She took a step back but her gaze never once left my face.

"You can tell those girls that if they ever try anything like that again, I won't be so understanding. And you—you'd better make sure you win the level two competition."

With that, she left me standing alone in the store room. It took me a few seconds to realise the rhythmic thumping noise was my heart. I'd done it. I'd got her to reverse the spell, but at what price? What would she do to me if I blew it in the Levels Competition? That was way too scary to even think about.

I rang Aunt Lucy and gave her the good news.

"They'll have to live with the ears for another two days though."

"Thanks, Jill. Hold on while I tell the girls."

I heard her call the twins, and then moments later—

"Thanks, Jill! Yay!"

"We owe you, Jill!"

"Did you hear that?" Aunt Lucy asked.

"Yeah. Tell them no more practical jokes on Grandma."

"Don't worry. They won't make that mistake again. I hope we didn't mess up your day."

"No, it's okay. I'm at Grandma's shop. There's a speed knitting competition between my PA, Mrs V, and her sister."

"Hmm. That sounds—" She hesitated, searching for the right word. "Exciting?"

"Yeah. Next week she's going to have the walls painted, and we're all going to watch them dry."

Aunt Lucy laughed. "Is your lady going to win?"

"Unlikely. Her sister seems to delight in beating Mrs V down."

"That's not very nice. I may be able to help. Listen—"

Chapter 11

As Mrs V and I were walking back to the office, she could hardly contain her delight.

"Did you see G's face?" She laughed.

"She didn't look happy."

"Now she knows what it feels like to lose."

"I thought there'd be a trophy or something for the winner," I said.

"I don't care about a trophy. Beating G is better than all the trophies in the world. Maybe now she'll be a little more humble."

"Do you really think so?"

"No. Not for more than a week or so anyway. Still, I don't care. Every time she starts bragging, I'll remind her of today."

"We should buy champagne."

"Not for me, thanks. I want to keep a clear head so I can savour every moment. Mind you, I didn't think I was going to win. With only thirty minutes to go, she was well ahead. I almost threw in the towel."

"You staged a great comeback."

"I did, didn't I?" Mrs V was bursting with pride. "Mind you, it helped that G kept dozing off in that last half hour. She must have pushed herself too hard."

"Definitely. Poor pacing if you ask me."

"It was still very close though."

"It must have been. That's why your sister asked for a re-measure."

"Still the same outcome." Mrs V smiled. "I took it by two inches. I just wished your grandmother had been there to see it."

"Yeah, it's a pity she got called away to do that TV interview. Still, I'm sure she'll be in touch to offer her congratulations. Where is your sister by the way?"

"She decided to go home early. Pity."

We both laughed.

Back at my flat, Mr Ivers looked in contemplative mood —
perhaps it was love.

"Evening, Mr Ivers."

"Oh, hello there."

"How's things?"

"Oh, you know. Same as usual. I have a double-bill of movies lined up for tomorrow."

"Will you be taking anyone with you?"

"No, I hadn't planned to, but if you're — "

"No, no. I thought maybe you and Betty — "

"The woman is a bore."

"Really?" Pot, kettle.

"All she talks about is sea shells. She spent two hours talking me through her collection. I couldn't wait to get out of there."

"Oh. I'm sorry." So much for my career as a matchmaker.

"You're welcome to come to the movies with me, Jill."

"Thanks, but I've got things to do — lots of things — important things. Got to rush, bye."

Two days later, Jackie Langford came to my office at ten o'clock, as arranged. I'd promised her an update on the 'Lift of Death' murder, but had precious little to tell her.

"I've viewed the CCTV. As reported in the press, there are no actual images of the murder itself. The only explanation I've been able to come up with so far, which makes any sense, is that Alan had already been stabbed when he stepped into the lift."

"Wouldn't the other people in the lift have noticed?"

"I would have expected them to, but apparently they didn't realise anything was wrong until he collapsed. I've spoken to all of the residents as well as some of the staff. To be perfectly honest with you, I'm no further along. All of the residents appear to keep themselves to themselves. There may be some kind of relationship between two of the single residents, but there's nothing to suggest that had any connection to the murder. There's also a question mark over how some of the residents can afford to live in a place like Tregar Court. I'm going to look a little more closely at that to see if it turns up anything of interest."

"Is there anything I can do to help?" Jackie said.

"Not really. Unless you remember anything else which Alan said or did which might help. Did he ever mention any of his neighbours? Or anything about Tregar Court, come to that?"

"He never talked about his neighbours, but he was always complaining about the building."

"Anything in particular?"

"All sorts of things. Nosey concierge, dirty common areas, that sort of thing. Nothing earth shattering, but when you're paying that kind of money, you expect the best. I must have told him a dozen times to find somewhere else. Heaven knows, he could have afforded to move."

"Why didn't he?"

"I don't know. Even though he hated the place at times, it seemed like he couldn't bring himself to leave. Men! I'll never understand them."

We talked for another thirty minutes, but neither of us

came up with anything new. Before she left, she made a fuss of Winky.

"He's such a little darling."

"You can have him if you like."

She laughed.

"Why can't you be more like her?" Winky said, after she'd left.

"She'd soon change her tune if she had to live with you."

He looked affronted. "You're the one who's difficult to live with. You should be grateful that I'm so easy-going."

Candlefield didn't do the Internet, so if I was going to find any information on The Dark One, I'd need to go old-school. When had I last been in a library? At school, probably. My teachers would have been ashamed of me.

Candlefield library looked and felt just like my school library. The only difference was that the 'no talking' rule was much more strictly enforced in Candlefield.

"Excuse me," I said.

"Shhh!" The witch, dressed in an overdose of floral print, put a finger to her lips. "How can I help?" she whispered.

"Where can I find archived copies of the newspapers?" I whispered back.

She beckoned me to follow her down a flight of stairs. The basement had no carpets, but no shortage of dust. I sneezed.

"Shhh!"

"Where are the readers?"

She looked puzzled.

"Microfiche readers?"

She shook her head. "We don't have those. All the original copies are stored down here."

"All of them?"

"This basement stretches for several miles under the town. There's a copy of every newspaper going back over a century."

"Are they in any kind of order?"

"Of course. No one would be able to find anything otherwise. They're stored by year with the most recent nearest to the stairs. Then they're divided into the different publications."

"How many different newspapers are there?"

"Each of the different sups has its own paper. For example, The Wonder is published by and for Wizards and Witches. Then there's The Candle which is a general publication. As you might imagine, it has the largest circulation. Is there anything else you need?"

Apart from a thousand pairs of eyes? "No, thank you."

"Please make sure you return everything to where you found it."

"I will."

I decided to discard those publications aimed at specific sup groups—the real news seemed to be concentrated in The Candle. I figured if I started with newspapers from ten years ago, and worked my way towards the present day, that I could make a note of all the incidents involving The Dark One.

Three hours later, I emerged from the basement—my nostrils coated in dust, and my hands in newsprint.

"Did you find what you were looking for?" Floral print whispered.

I shook my head and tried not to sneeze. "I couldn't find a

single article on The Dark One."

"You should have said that's what you were looking for. I could have saved you a lot of time."

"Why aren't there any stories about him?"

She shrugged. "You should ask the newspapers that question."

I intended to, but first I had an appointment with a cup of coffee and a muffin at Cuppy C.

"Blueberry!" I could barely control my joy. "You have blueberry."

"It was the least we could do." Pearl handed me the tray. "After what you did for us." She touched a finger to her ear. "Grab the window seat; I'll come and join you in a minute."

Amber beat her to it.

"Nice?" Amber said.

I nodded — my mouth was too full to speak.

"Thanks for what you did with Grandma."

I shrugged.

Pearl joined us. "How did you get Grandma to reverse the spell?"

"I relied on reason and her sense of fair play."

They both laughed. "No, seriously. How did you manage it?"

"I told her that I wouldn't take part in her stupid Levels Competition."

Their mouths fell open.

"What?" I shrugged.

"Nothing," Pearl said. "I just can't believe you're still in one piece."

"I'm surprised she didn't turn you into a frog — or a

donkey," Amber said. "She must want to win really badly."

"That's what worries me. What chance do I have of winning? I've only just moved up from level one. Surely even Grandma will have to make allowances?"

They both shook their heads.

"Thanks. That makes me feel much better."

"You'll win." Amber put her hand on mine. "You're the best level two witch I've ever seen."

"Yeah, you'll win." Pearl added her hand.

I wished I shared their confidence. It's not like there wouldn't be enough pressure going into the competition anyway, but now I had the threat of being transformed into a donkey, hanging over me.

"Did you enjoy that?" Amber asked, after I'd scooped up the last few crumbs.

"It was delicious."

"Good. Now we have another favour to ask you."

"You two have used up all your favours."

"Don't forget we got blueberry muffins for you."

"Does this favour involve Grandma?"

"No. I promise. It's just that it's our birthday next week."

"Are you having a joint party?"

"That's just it. We thought—" Amber looked at her sister.

"Yeah, we were thinking—" Pearl said.

I had a horrible feeling I knew where this was heading.

"We'd really like to go to Washbridge for our birthday."

"Shopping?"

"No, we thought we could go out for the evening."

"For a meal?"

"No, silly. Going out for meals is for old people. We want to go to a club. To dance."

"I'm sure I'll be able to come up with somewhere for you to go."

"You have to come too," Pearl said.

"Me? No, I'm old people."

"Don't be silly. You're not old. Kathy can come too."

Yay! Can't wait.

"So, can we?" Amber had the pathetic puppy dog face off to a tee.

"Please!" So did Pearl.

"Okay. I'll see what I can arrange." What else could I have done?

"Thanks, Jill. You're the best!"

I timed my visit to Kathy's so the kids would be at school.

"Hello, stranger," Kathy had a cheese cracker in her mouth. "Come in. Coffee?"

"No, thanks. I'm not stopping."

"I saw your grandma's shop on Wool TV the other day."

"Since when did you watch Wool TV?"

"I heard about the competition on the radio, so thought I'd check it out. Exciting finish wasn't it?"

"Thrilling."

"I thought you'd be pleased that Mrs V won."

"I am. She deserved to get one over on her sister."

"What brings you here? Come to see the new beanie creations?"

"You're sick. It's a wonder Child Protection haven't taken the kids away."

"It's creative. That kangadillo is a work of genius."

"Of a sick mind more like. Anyway, that's not why I'm here. It's the twins' birthday next week. They want to come to Washbridge and go to a club."

"Good for them."

"They want us to go with them."

"Are you sure you can manage a late night? Don't you have to be tucked up in bed by ten?"

"You make me sound old," I said.

"You act old."

"Rubbish! So, are you up for it?"

"Just try stopping me. It's ages since I got down and funky."

"I don't think anyone gets down and funky any more – if they ever did. Look, you don't have to go. Are you sure you wouldn't like more time to think about it?"

"I'm in. I'll have to buy a new dress though."

"Like you need an excuse."

"Anyway, I've got news too," Kathy said.

"Does it involve the wilful destruction of beanies?"

"When I was listening to the radio, there was a phone-in competition. You'll never guess who won."

"The kangadillo?"

"No. Me! Guess *what* I won."

"A trillion pounds?"

"Close. A voucher for a manicure and pedicure." She grinned inanely. "For two!"

"Don't look at me." I shook my head. "No! No way."

"It'll be great."

"I can't have anyone touching my feet." I shuddered at the thought.

"We can get our nails done for the twins' birthday night out. I'll book us in."

Chapter 12

"You have a visitor," Mrs V whispered when I arrived at the office.

"Who?"

"Your grandmother. She doesn't look happy."

When did she ever?

"Morning, Grandma. To what do I owe this unexpected pleasure?"

"I'm on to you." She pointed a crooked finger at me – at least I think it was at me – it was hard to tell.

"What have I done now?"

"Don't come the innocent with me, missy. You used the 'sleep' spell on Mrs G."

"How can you even suggest such a thing? You would have known if I had."

"You're right. I would have known – IF I'D BEEN THERE. But I was at the TV studios for an interview – THAT NO ONE KNEW ANYTHING ABOUT!"

"Oh dear. I wonder how that could have happened. There must have been some kind of mix up."

"Your mother was just the same." Grandma snorted. "Thought she knew it all. Thought she was clever. Looks like the apple didn't fall far from the tree."

"I wonder who she got it from."

I really should learn when to keep my mouth shut. For instance, when Grandma's wart began to glow red would have been a good time to stay quiet.

"You'd better win the Levels, or you'll be sorry." With that she stomped out of my office, slamming the door closed behind her.

Winky came out from under my desk where he'd been

hiding while Grandma went off on one. "I wouldn't like to see her when she's angry. Sounds to me like you are in her bad books."

"When aren't I?"

It was at times like this that I was pleased Mrs V was a little on the deaf side. I wouldn't have wanted her to find out that I'd used a little magic to *'assist'* her win.

The Tregar case was getting under my skin—nothing made sense. How and when had Alan Dennis been stabbed? There was no sign of the attack taking place during that last, fateful lift ride. He'd been standing at the very front, which meant that only his head and shoulders were visible on CCTV, so it was possible he'd already been stabbed before he entered the lift. But surely the other people in the lift would have noticed if he'd been bleeding. Or would they? No one in that apartment block seemed very interested in their neighbours. By their own admission, they all kept themselves to themselves. Was it possible that they had all been so involved with their own thoughts that they hadn't noticed the man was bleeding? In the absence of any other bright ideas, that was the theory I was working on.

I intended to do more digging around into the backgrounds of Jason Allan and Darcy James—I wanted to know why they'd denied knowing one another when all the evidence suggested otherwise. More importantly, I wanted to know how they could afford to live at Tregar Court.

It wasn't difficult to trace previous addresses for them. Darcy James didn't stay in one place for long—I had a list of five previous addresses for her. By contrast, there was only one previous address for Jason Allan. My curiosity was piqued because that address was in one of the most run-down areas of Washbridge. It was hard to imagine how anyone could have gone straight from there to Tregar Court — maybe he'd won the lottery?

The Sunnyside estate had the highest crime rate in Washbridge. If newspaper reports were to be believed (were they ever?), it had become a virtual no-go area for the police. Fortunately, the address I needed was close to the edge of the estate. I didn't want to risk getting back to the car to find it minus its wheels, so I parked half a mile away and made my way on foot. When the estate had first been built, over half a century before, it had been considered state of the art. Those days were now long gone. Most of the houses were in dire need of repair, and many were empty — boarded up to deter squatters. I soon found the address I was looking for. The ground floor windows and door had been boarded up — the upstairs windows were all broken. No one had lived there for some considerable time. From the gate, I saw movement in the ground floor window of the adjoining property. I waved to catch their attention.

"Sorry to trouble you," I said when the neighbour came out into the garden.

"It's no trouble, dear." The old woman's slippers looked two sizes too big for her. "Are you looking for someone?"

"The Allan family."

"They're long gone. I was just about to make a cuppa. Care to join me?"

"Thanks. That would be nice."

Mrs Deirdre Downs made a remarkably good cup of tea, but the real bonus came when she offered me a custard cream straight out of the packet. The interior of her house was very seventies, and spotlessly clean.

"Did you know the Allans?"

"Me and Gina were good friends. We both moved in about the same time. Our kids used to play together."

"You knew Jason then?"

"Yeah. Funny lad. Harmless though. He was a carpet fitter, I think. Stayed with his mother right until she died — cancer — poor thing."

"Did Gina have any other children?"

"A girl — Sarah. A bit lippy, but a good heart."

"What about the father?"

"*Fathers*. Gina was pregnant with Jason when she moved here. I never did get the full story on what happened with *his* dad. Gina had Sarah with Benny. He died a few years before Gina — heart attack."

"So Jason lived here until his mother died?"

She nodded. "Yeah, don't know what happened to him then. He just seemed to disappear. I hope he's all right."

"He's alive and well. Do you have any idea where I might find his sister?"

"She lives on the Pleaston estate, I think. Done all right for herself."

Not as well as Jason apparently.

"Her name's Sarah Conway now," Deirdre said. "She married a nice young man. Civil servant I believe."

Twenty minutes and two more custard creams later, I thanked her, and set off back to the car.

I'd only gone a few hundred yards when I found my way blocked by three teenagers. The ringleader was a girl, who looked no more than seventeen. All tattoos and piercings, she spoke through a mouthful of gum. Her male sidekicks, Little and Large, were criminally ugly.

"Get out of my way please," I said.

"Give us your phone and your money or he'll cut you." Tattoos gestured to Little who drew a knife.

"I asked you to get out of my way."

Little took a step towards me, so I cast the 'illusion' spell. He dropped the knife like a hot potato.

"What's up wi' you?" she shouted at her henchman.

"It—I—Err." The poor guy was staring at what appeared to him to be a snake.

Large stepped forward. His knife was longer than his cohort's, but he dropped it just as quickly.

"Pick 'em up!" she screamed.

The two boys were transfixed—too scared to approach the snakes.

"Get out the way!" she screamed in frustration. As she stooped to pick up one of the knives, I cast the 'illusion' spell for a third time. Tattoos fell onto her backside as she reeled away from the snakes.

The three of them were still staring at the knives as I strolled past them. I'd be at my car by the time the spells wore off.

Mrs V was still glowing from the victory over her sister. It had been worth the risk of being on the receiving end of Grandma's wrath to see Mrs V so happy.

"A man came here while you were out." Mrs V was knitting a pink sock today. "He wanted to look around and take measurements. I told him he'd have to speak to you first."

"It wasn't Maurice Montage again, was it?"

"No. he didn't give his name. He just said he'd come back later."

"Okay. How is the Everlasting Wool working out?"

"It's fine. The problem is that my subscription only allows me to use a single colour. Not that I'm complaining because it didn't cost me anything. If you want to use more colours though, you have to increase your monthly payments."

Clever. Grandma reels them in with a low opening offer, and then upsells them when they're hooked.

Winky was on the window sill, flags in hand. I thought he'd abandoned the semaphore.

"Morning, cat. How's the love life?"

He ignored me—too busy waving his flags around.

"I'm fine, Jill," I answered myself. "Thank you for asking. How are you?"

Winky gave me a one-eyed look of disdain.

"Thank you for asking, Winky. I'm fine too."

"They'll lock you away if you keep talking to yourself," Winky said, still signalling with his flags.

"Whereas, talking to a cat—totally sane."

Winky dropped the flags, jumped down from the window sill, and onto my desk.

"Don't you dare scratch it!" I screamed.

"I need your help." He fixed me with his one eye.

"The answer is no."

"You don't even know what I'm going to ask."

"I am not having the office re-imagined."

"I know that. I was just messing with your head. Bella has asked me over on a date."

"Bella, the neighbourhood flirt?"

"That was all a misunderstanding. It's just her and me now. She has invited me for dinner, but I'll need you to take me over there."

"What about her owners?"

"Owners? No one *owns* her."

"Look, what I mean is. It's like you and me —"

"Exactly. I chose you *ergo* I'm in charge. Same for Bella."

"Ergo?"

"It's Latin."

"You speak Latin?"

"Doesn't everyone? Look I need you to take me over there. Okay?"

"Sure, why not?" At least then one of us would have a love life.

Some days it felt like I was living in a kind of parallel universe.

"That man is back," Mrs V said. "The one who called earlier — the one who wanted to look around."

"You'd better show him in."

"Ms Gooder. Thank you for seeing me."

I had an irrational distrust of any man who wore a handkerchief in the breast pocket of his jacket.

"My name is Gordon Armitage."

Despite my reservations vis-a-vis the handkerchief, I shook his hand.

"Ms Gooder, I wanted to —"

"Call me Jill, please."

"And you must call me Gordon."

"What can I do for you, Gordon?"

"You've no doubt seen our offices, next door. Armitage, Armitage, Armitage and Poole."

"Yes, I think so. Which one are you?"

"Sorry?"

"Armitage, Armitage or Armitage?"

"The first one."

Winky chose that moment to jump onto the window sill.

"You have a cat?" Armitage did a double-take.

"That's Winky."

"He's only got one—"

"Eye, yes. Hence the name."

"Winky." He laughed. "Of course. Funny."

"So how can I help you, Gordon?"

"Our practice is growing quite rapidly, and the truth is, we're running out of space. We need to expand."

I had a fair idea where this conversation was headed, but decided to play dumb. "I'm still not sure how I can help."

"The obvious move would be for us to expand into the building next door."

"This one?"

"Precisely."

"I see a minor flaw in your plan, Gordon. I'm already here, and there are two other businesses in this building."

"We've already come to an agreement with the others. They're going to relocate, and in return we will recompense them generously. That's why I wanted to talk to you."

"I'm sorry to disappoint you, but I've no intention of relocating. This was my father's office—"

"A sentimental attachment. I can understand that. Still, I'm sure for the right figure—"

"Sorry. I'm here to stay. You'll have to rethink your expansion plans. There's a larger property over the road which is standing empty. Maybe you should check that out."

"Name your figure." Gordon's cheery disposition had disappeared.

"I don't have a figure. I have no interest in moving."

"I'm sorry to hear that." He glanced at Winky. "Does the landlord know that you are keeping animals on the premises?"

"It's been a pleasure, Gordon." I walked over to the door, and opened it. "But I'd like you to leave now."

"You'll be hearing from me again," he said as he left.

"Looking forward to it."

"What did he want?" Mrs V asked.

"He's from next door. He wants us out so they can expand into this building."

"What did you tell him?"

"To do one."

Chapter 13

It was the twins' birthday and, as arranged, they were going to come over to Washbridge to celebrate. Tonight, we were going clubbing—yay, joy of joys. But before that, Kathy and I were going for a manicure and pedicure—yay again! Could this day get any worse?

"Morning, Jill."
Yes, apparently it could.
"Morning, Betty. Lovely day."
"The sun doesn't agree with me," she said.
That would explain the parka.
"Aren't you hot in that?"
"It's better than the alternative. I blister."
"Nasty."
She glanced around furtively. "I'm trying to avoid that man."
"Who?"
"Mr Ivers. I don't know how you put up with him. He's such a bore. He never stops talking about the movies he's seen."
"Pity, I thought you and he might hit it off."
"Certainly not. He even tried to sign me up for his stupid newsletter. Who'd be crazy enough to pay for that?"
Who indeed?
"He did give me an idea though," she said, still keeping a lookout for the man in question.
"Oh?"
"I got to thinking. If he can sell his boring cinema newsletter, then I'm sure I could produce a newsletter on sea shells."

"Is there a lot of sea shell related news?"

"You'd be surprised."

Gobsmacked, more like.

"You could be my first subscriber."

Before I could enjoy the delights of the nail bar, I had to pay a visit to Sarah Conway. The Pleaston estate was certainly no Tregar Court, but it was a massive step up from Sunnyside.

Sarah, who had a young baby, was only too happy to talk to me about her family.

"Jason and I don't keep in touch. We haven't spoken for—" She did a calculation on her fingers. "Must be over six years now. We were never particularly close even when we were kids."

"Did you know he was living in Tregar Court?"

"Yeah. Someone told me a couple of years ago. I didn't believe them at first."

"Look, this is kind of a sensitive question, but do you have any idea how he can afford to live there?"

"Not a clue. Last I heard he was fitting carpets."

"Is it possible he came into money? Could he have won the lottery or something?"

"That's the only explanation I could come up with. He wouldn't have told me if he had."

"Is there anyone who might have left him money? In a Will?"

"I wouldn't have thought so."

"What about his father?"

"I never knew Jason's dad. Neither did he. He'd done a runner before Jason was born."

"Do you know why he left?"

"Not really. Mum didn't like to talk about it. I do know that Mum and Jason's dad used to live in a much nicer part of Washbridge, but that was before Jason was born. There were money problems of some sort. That's why Mum ended up moving to Sunnyside."

"Do you have any idea where Jason's father might be?"

"No. He and Mum never married, so I never even knew his name. I do have a photo of him and Mum taken a few years before he did a bunk."

"Could I see it?"

"Sure. It's in the spare bedroom. I'll go get it. Watch Courtney for me will you?"

What? Leave me alone in charge of a baby? Was she insane?

Courtney looked up at me and gurgled.

"Hello, I'm Jill."

She burped. I had that effect on people.

Ten minutes later, Sarah returned with an old metal tin.

"It's in here somewhere."

She emptied the photos out onto the coffee table. The majority of them were of her and Jason through the ages.

"There you go." She handed me the faded, black and white photograph.

Even though the man was many years younger in the photo, I recognised him immediately.

"Why can't I just have a manicure?" I said, as Kathy led me by the arm.

"Because I won a combined manicure and pedicure. I don't want to waste my prize."

"But I hate anyone touching my feet."

"When exactly was the last time anyone touched your

feet?"

"I don't remember, but just the thought of it gives me the creeps."

"Tough. You're going to have a manicure *and* pedicure, and you're going to like it. Got it?"

Sisters. Anyone want one?

'Nailed It' was in the Greenlands shopping mall. Have I mentioned how much I hate malls? Soulless, sterile and boring—all of them. Kathy worshipped at the altar of the mall. Given half a chance, she'd have moved in. No class, my sister.

I'd hoped I might accidentally on purpose get lost in the crowds and sneak away, but Kathy had my number. She only released my arm once we were inside 'Nailed It'.

The interior was a shade of turquoise which reminded me of my mouthwash. Behind the semicircular counter was an army of manicurists all sporting identical black smocks. On our side of the counter sat a number of women ranging in ages from a giddy teenager to a woman who looked almost as old as Grandma.

"Morning ladies."

I recognised that voice. Daze gave me a wink.

"Welcome to Nailed It. How can I help?"

What was she doing here? Daze, whose real name was Daisy Flowers, was a super supernatural or sup sup for short. She worked as a Rogue Retriever which meant she brought back rogue supernaturals from the human world. She was one tough cookie and apparently now a manicurist. In the short time I'd known her, she'd worked behind the counter in a fast food restaurant, been a parking warden and now this. Versatile or what?

"I called earlier and made a booking. And we have

vouchers." Kathy held up her prized possessions. "I won them in a local radio phone-in."

"Congratulations," Daze said with way too much enthusiasm. "These entitle you to the combined manicure and pedicure. For two."

"Yay!" Kathy squealed. She really was that excited. Weirdo.

"Lucinda will be your manicurist today." She pointed towards a petite brunette at the far end of the counter.

Kathy made her way over to the waiting Lucinda.

"And I will be yours," Daze said, as she led me in the opposite direction.

"You don't have to do this," I whispered, as we took our seats on opposite sides of the narrow counter. "I didn't want to come anyway."

"Of course I must. I don't want to blow my cover." Daze took out a small plastic box containing all manner of hand grooming paraphernalia. "Anyway. I'm rather good at it, if I do say so myself."

That's when I spotted her name badge, and laughed.

"What?"

"Nothing, sorry."

"What are you laughing at?"

Whoops. Golden survival rule number one: don't cross Grandma. Golden survival rule number two: don't upset Daze.

"It's just—err—the name badge."

"Oh, that thing. It wasn't my idea. They wouldn't let me use 'Daze'."

"Daisy is a nice name."

I didn't like the way she was looking at me. And I especially didn't like the way the nail file was pointing towards my throat.

"Not for you, obviously. For someone else—someone who was more 'daisy like'."

Much to my surprise, the manicure wasn't the ordeal I'd expected. Not that I was any kind of expert, but Daze did appear to know what she was doing.

"Whoaaa!!" I almost jumped out of the chair.

"What's the matter?" Daze looked concerned.

"How did you do that?"

"What?"

"Clip my toe nail?"

"I didn't."

Both of her hands were in plain view, so who was touching my feet? I peered under the counter.

"Blaze?"

"Hi," he squeaked.

"Hi."

Blaze was Daze's sidekick and apprentice Rogue Retriever.

"Does he know what he's doing?" I whispered to Daze.

"He's a wiz when it comes to feet."

I certainly hoped so.

"What are you guys really working on?"

Daze handed me a swatch of colours to choose from.

"There's a rogue werewolf in the district. We need to get him before the full moon tomorrow."

"Anything I can do to help?"

"No, thanks. We got this one. Have you had any joy with your TDO investigations?"

"Not really. I couldn't find a single article in the newspapers about The Dark One. Why do you think that is? Are the press afraid?"

"Possibly. Have you decided on a colour?"

I flicked through the swatch, and selected the most neutral shade I could find. "This one will do."

"Not very adventurous."

"I have enough adventure in my life already."

Kathy had chosen the polar opposite of neutral.

"What colour is that?" I pointed to her toe nails.

"It's called 'purple dazzle'. Do you like it?"

"It's very—purple."

"What do you think of these?" She held out her hands.

"Greentastic!"

"Green and purple?"

"I wasn't sure they'd work, but I'm really pleased with them. Haven't they done yours yet?"

"Yeah, look." I held out my hand.

She looked confused.

"It's called 'shades of neutral'."

"You're so boring, Jill. Are your toes the same?"

"Of course."

She sighed. "What time are the twins coming over?"

"Six o'clock."

"Are they going straight to your place?"

After their last visit, it had taken me a week to get the flat back to normal. I wasn't going to make that mistake again.

"No, they're going to meet us outside Ever A Wool Moment. They wanted to have a look around Grandma's shop before we meet up with them."

"We've got a few hours to kill then."

"Don't you have to get back for the kids?"

"No. Pete's taken a day's holiday. He's taking the kids to the cinema. I have the whole day to myself. So, what shall we do?"

Much as I loved Kathy. I could only take her in small doses. I had assumed I'd be able to fit in a little work in between the nail bar and meeting up with the twins. So much for that plan.

"There is *one* thing I have to do," I said.

"It had better not be work. This is a holiday."

"It's not work exactly, but I do have to call in at the office."

Kathy scowled.

"Honestly, it isn't work. You'll see."

Mrs V's 'washing line' was strung across the outer office. Kathy and I had to duck underneath the socks to get to her desk.

"I see you're into socks now, Mrs V," Kathy said.

"Yes, I'm getting better at them. I wanted to hang them up so people can see them properly."

"What about would-be clients?" I asked.

"It's okay. They won't damage the socks if they duck underneath."

That's okay then.

At Mrs V's invitation, Kathy picked out socks for Peter and the kids. While she was making her selection, I sneaked into my office.

"I thought you'd forgotten me," Winky said.

"As if. Your love life is my top priority right now."

"Sarcasm does not become you. Get the basket."

"Where are we taking that ugly thing?" Kathy was putting the socks into a small plastic bag.

"It's not a 'thing', it's a 'he'. And he's not ugly."

"Where are we taking 'he'?"

"I—err—I have to drop him off somewhere."

"Vets?"

"No. Just across the road actually."

"Why?"

So many questions. What was I meant to say? That Winky had a date with Bella? That they'd arranged it via semaphore?

"We take turns cat-sitting."

Mrs V gave me a puzzled look. This was obviously news to her.

"It's a new arrangement."

To avoid any more awkward Winky-related questions, I ducked under the washing line and made my way out.

"You wait here," I said to Kathy, when we reached the building where Bella lived.

She shrugged. "Hurry up then. I'm starving."

"Where am I supposed to leave you?" I whispered to Winky.

"Flat twenty-five. Just ring the doorbell, and leave me outside."

The concierge gave me the kind of look you'd expect from someone who'd just seen me talking to a cat.

"Are you sure?"

"I know what I'm doing."

Good thing one of us does.

I was convinced the concierge would intercept me as I made my way to the lifts. He didn't, but his gaze followed me every step of the way.

"Shouldn't I wait until someone answers the door?"

"No, just ring the bell, and go."

I did as instructed and then legged it back to the lift.

Another *oh so normal* day in my *oh so normal* life.

Chapter 14

Kathy wanted to visit a cocktail bar before we met up with the twins, but I refused point blank. The night was going to be difficult enough as it was without getting drunk so early in the evening. I suggested we get coffee and a snack.

"What's wrong with you, Jill?"

"What do you mean?"

"Are you allergic to having fun?"

What did she mean? I could do 'fun'. "I don't see what's fun about getting drunk."

"We don't have to get drunk. Just something to take the edge off."

"Like on your birthday?" That was a low blow considering it had been my 'sleep' spell, and not the drink, which had knocked her out on her birthday — the last time we were out together.

"Just take a look at yourself, Jill. You're young. You're single. And yet, you never seem to have any fun. No wonder you can't get a guy."

"That's not fair. Who says I can't get a guy?"

"You know what I mean. I'm married with kids, but I still know how to have a good time. YOLO."

"Yo what?"

"YOLO. You Only Live Once."

"Where do you come up with these stupid acronyms?"

"Everyone uses them. Everyone apart from you, apparently."

"Can I help it if I like to speak in English?"

"No more than you can help being boring."

"I am *not* boring! I know how to let my hair down. I can

be just as wild as the next person." There, that had told her. "Now, come on, the library is just around the corner."

"Are you kidding me? Is that your idea of letting your hair down?"

"There's a coffee shop in the basement. They have cupcakes."

"You really do like to walk on the wild side, don't you?"

I ignored Kathy's moans and groans as I led the way through the library.

"Hold on," she said, just as I was about to take the stairs to the basement.

I flinched when I saw her studying the noticeboard which was full of flyers from reading groups and amateur dramatics clubs.

"I'm not going to any more am-dram productions." I'd had my fill of bad scripts and acting for one year.

"Look!" She pointed a 'greentastic' nail at a small white sheet of paper in among the more colourful flyers. "What do you think?"

"What do I think about what?"

"This job. The hours would be ideal for me."

"Since when were you looking for a job?"

The notice gave details of a part-time vacancy for someone to stack shelves with the books that had been returned.

"I need something to do now the kids are both at school. I'm going stir crazy stuck in the house all day with nothing to do."

"What about the housework?"

"You sound like Pete. I need to get out. I need to do something more exciting than housework."

"Do you really think that stacking books would be

exciting?"

"At least I'd get out of the house. Plus I'd get to talk to other people."

"You talk to me."

"Yeah, but you don't count. And besides, you're boring. It doesn't matter anyway, I'm too late." Kathy sighed. "Applications had to be in last Friday."

Over coffee and cupcakes, Kathy continued to bemoan her boring life.

"I love the kids to bits. And Pete. But I need something more. Something for me."

I nodded.

"I could work for you," she said.

Whoa! Where had that come from? "Work for me?"

"Yeah. Why not? Not so much *for* you as *with* you. I could help with your investigations. Go undercover—that kind of thing."

"I don't think so."

"Why not? I'd make a great P.I. If *you* can do it, how difficult can it be?"

"Gee, thanks."

"You know what I mean. I could follow people and stuff."

"My job description to a tee: *I follow people and stuff.* Anyway, I couldn't pay you. I barely make enough to pay myself."

"You could sack Mrs V."

"Wow! I thought I was supposed to be the one who lacked compassion."

"She's old. She'd thank you for it."

"No she wouldn't. She loves her job, and besides, I don't pay her."

"What? Why not?"

"It wasn't my idea for her to work for free. I told her I couldn't afford to keep her on, but she insisted she wanted to stay anyway."

"That's no good. I'm not working for nothing."

I was gutted. "Oh, well."

"Will you keep an eye out for me? Let me know if you see anything that might be suitable?"

"Of course." The next time I saw an ad for a cocktail taster or a personal shopper, I'd be sure to let her know.

Ever A Wool Moment was quieter than usual. At least it was in terms of customer numbers. Volume-wise, it was way noisier than usual thanks to the twins.

Grandma met me and Kathy at the door. "Get the twins out of here. They're scaring away the customers."

"Hello, Grandma." I treated her to my most insincere smile. "This is my sister, Kathy."

Kathy held out a hand which Grandma ignored. "They've been at the cocktails." She nodded in the direction of Amber and Pearl who seemed way too happy just at being in a wool shop.

"Lucky them," Kathy said.

"Jill!" Pearl screamed when she caught sight of me.

"Kathy, hi!" Amber shouted.

The twins rushed across the shop, knocking over a display of knitting needles as they did, and then threw their arms around us.

"Happy birthday, you two," I said.

"Thanks, Jill. And thanks for the cards and presents!"

Grandma cleared her throat. The wart on the end of her nose was throbbing red. A danger sign if ever there was one.

"Maybe we should get going," I said.

"Wait!" Kathy stepped forward.

I followed her gaze and saw the small card taped to the inside of the shop window: 'Part-time sales assistant wanted.'

"I could do that," Kathy said.

"No!" I'd said before I could stop myself.

"Why not?" She turned on me.

"Yes, why not?" Grandma had found a grin from somewhere. "Why couldn't your sister do that?"

"Well — because — err"

"We're waiting," Grandma said. "Why not?"

"She doesn't have any experience. With wool I mean. She can't knit for toffee."

"*Thanks*, Jill." Kathy looked daggers at me.

"No experience necessary," Grandma cackled.

"She has kids. She'd have to be home in time to collect them from school." I was clutching at straws now.

"No problem." Grandma was enjoying this way too much. "The hours are flexible. I'm sure we can work around that. When could you start?"

"Next week?"

"Next week would be fine."

"Yay! I got a job," Kathy said, as we walked down the street.

"Yay!" I said with no enthusiasm at all.

"Are you sure you want to work for Grandma?" Amber said.

"She can be quite brutal." Pearl chimed in.

"If I can manage two kids, I'm sure I can handle her." Kathy was over the moon.

The twins and I exchanged a glance. None of us had the heart to enlighten the poor, delusional fool.

Three hours, and several cocktail bars later, we arrived at Tremors—Washbridge's newest, and loudest club. The twins and Kathy were now the wrong side of 'merry'. I was still stone-cold sober, having refused or disposed of the various ridiculously named cocktails that had been foisted upon me. Someone had to keep their wits about them, and as usual, that job had fallen to me—little Miss Boring.

I'm pretty useless at dancing, but that night, I was the best in our small group. Kathy, who when sober, was actually quite the mover, was now an uncoordinated mess of arms and legs. And yet, even she was better than the twins. Sup dancing was very different to human dancing. Think of synchronised swimming, but without the water, and you'll get a vague idea of what passes for dancing among sups.

"What on earth are the twins doing?" Kathy slurred into my ear.

I shrugged. I simply didn't have words to describe it. Within fifteen minutes of the twins stepping onto the dance floor, they were the only ones left on there. Everyone else had formed a circle around the edge—looking on in disbelief.

Amber and Pearl—seemingly oblivious to the attention they'd attracted—ramped things up to the next level. Now, it's entirely possible that in Candlefield, their routine would have gone down a storm, but not in Washbridge.

"What's up with them two?" A slim redhead with entirely

too much bust pointed a finger towards the twins.

"Looks like they're having a seizure." Her friend with big eyebrows and an overdose of lip gloss laughed.

The twins ignored the jibes at first, but the redhead and her friend had more where that came from. They threw one insult after another at the twins, much to the delight of the crowd who joined in the laughter.

"Come on." I grabbed the twins by their arms, and led them off the dance floor and over to the far side of the room where it was a little quieter. In my rush to get them away, I'd lost Kathy somewhere.

"Why were they so horrible?" Amber wiped a tear away.

"We were only dancing." Pearl looked on the verge of tears too.

"That's not how we dance here," I said.

Amber shot me a look. I hadn't realised what I'd said until it was too late. I never should have used the word 'we'.

"Sorry, I meant humans. They don't dance like that."

"Like what?" Pearl sobbed.

"Like—" I didn't want to rub salt in the wounds. "Like you were dancing just now."

"We're good dancers!" Amber said.

"I know. It's just that—well it isn't how humans dance." I turned back to the dance floor which was now full again. "Look."

The twins stared at the dance floor, then at each other, and then at me. "You call that dancing?" Pearl said.

"They're just waving their hands around." Amber shrugged. "What's so good about that?"

"Nothing I guess. It's just what we—err—humans do."

"It's rubbish." Pearl was more angry than upset now.

"It's boring." Amber was annoyed too. "And why did

they have to be so mean anyway?" She was glaring at the redhead and her friend who were now strutting their stuff on the dance floor.

"Ignore them. I'd better go and find Kathy. You two stay right here." They were so intent on the dance floor, I wasn't sure they'd heard me. "Amber? Pearl? Stay here." They nodded.

It took me a few minutes to track Kathy down. I heard her before I saw her. Unfortunately, she's one of those people who think they can sing—but can't. Not even a little bit. It's bad enough when she's sober, but when she's drunk it's one hundred times worse.

"Kathy!" I called from the edge of the dance floor. "Kathy!"

"Come and dance!" She held up her hand, spilling half of her cocktail onto the dance floor as she did.

"We have to go!" I shouted over the music.

"Don't be daft. Come on. Come and have a dance!"

"We have to go right now. I think the twins might do something stupid—"

I heard the collective gasp, and knew immediately that I was too late. Kathy seemed oblivious to the commotion behind her.

I pushed through the crowd to find the redhead and her friend standing naked in the centre of the dance floor. Everyone laughed and pointed as the two girls desperately tried to cover themselves with their hands. I glanced around and caught sight of the twins on the opposite side of the room. They looked very pleased with their handiwork.

It took me a while to fight my way over to them.

"Reverse it!" I yelled at them.

"What?" Amber gave me a 'butter wouldn't melt' look.

"If you don't reverse it this instant, I'll never let you visit me again."

"They were horrible to us." Pearl pouted.

"I know they were, and now you've been horrible right back, but it ends now. Reverse it!"

The twins looked at one another, then back at me, and then reversed the spell.

The redhead and her friend—now fully clothed—pushed their way off the dance floor and made their way to the exit.

"What just happened?" someone said.

"They were naked, and then they weren't," another voice said.

"You're drunk!"

Hopefully the whole episode would be put down to a mass hallucination fuelled by drink—although I wasn't sure what the redhead and her friend would make of it when they woke the next morning.

Chapter 15

This hadn't been part of the plan.

After we'd escaped Tremors, I'd wanted to call it a night, but the twins and Kathy would have none of it. Instead of going home to a nice warm bath and a mug of hot chocolate, I'd been dragged around a succession of noisy, sweaty and generally unpleasant clubs. After studying the humans-at-dance, the twins had soon picked up on what passed as acceptable dance moves. They and Kathy had spent the whole night drinking and dancing while I'd played nanny to them. I had hoped the twins would go back to Candlefield, and that Kathy would go home to Peter. Best laid plans and all that. The three of them had all ended up back at my place. I'd had to call Peter and tell him that Kathy wouldn't be home until the next morning.

"This happens every time she goes out with you, Jill," he'd said before hanging up on me—like it was somehow my fault.

The three of them were still fast asleep on the living room floor when I got up the next morning. What? You didn't actually think I was going to let them mess up my spare bedroom again did you? Besides, the state those three had been in when we got home, they wouldn't have known where they were sleeping. All the way home in the taxi, Kathy had kept going on about the naked dancers in Tremors. The twins had been asleep, and I'd pretended not to know what she was talking about.

"What time is it?" Kathy opened one eye as I stepped over the prone bodies.

"Eight o'clock."

"What happened last night?"

"You got drunk."

"My head is splitting."

"Good. It's what you deserve."

I fed her two paracetamol, and told her to go back to sleep. Before leaving, I scribbled a short note for the three of them:

'Gone to work.

Help yourselves to breakfast.

Don't make a mess!'

I cast a spell to transport myself to Candlefield, and called in on Aunt Lucy.

"Morning, Jill. How are the girls?"

"Err — they're — still asleep."

"Did they get drunk last night?"

"Not really."

"You don't have to cover for them. It was their birthday, so I guess they're allowed. I hope they didn't make fools of themselves."

"No. Of course not."

If I'd let on that they'd used magic in the club, the twins would be in serious trouble. Sups were not meant to do anything which might give themselves away to humans.

"Did they see Grandma's shop?"

"Yes, but she kicked them out for getting too rowdy."

"After the donkey ears incident, I'd have thought that those girls would have learned their lesson."

"Grandma has offered Kathy a job in the shop."

"You don't sound very thrilled about the idea."

"I don't trust Grandma. I think she's up to something."

"Do you want me to have a word with her?"

"No. Let's see what happens. Maybe I'm being unfair."

Who was I kidding? That old witch was definitely up to something.

"How's Lester?" I said.

Aunt Lucy shrugged.

"I haven't seen him for a while."

"You and me both. I guess he must have lost interest." She forced a smile, but I could hear the sadness in her voice.

Eddie Lingard lived on the other side of the park where I'd first met Drake. He shared a house with two other people, one of whom answered the door.

"Can I help?" The young witch eyed me suspiciously.

"I'm looking for Eddie Lingard."

"Don't I know you?" She stared at me so intently it was a little unnerving. "Aren't you the one who found the Candlefield Cup?"

I nodded.

"I'm Sasha." Her face lit up and she offered me her hand. "I've heard a lot about you."

"Really?"

"Are you taking part in the Levels?"

"It's looking that way."

"Me too."

"What level are you?" I thought I should at least appear to be interested.

"Level two. Same as you. It's going to be a tough competition."

"I don't expect to do very well. I've only just moved up to that level."

"That's not what I hear. The talk is that you're the favourite."

"Me?" I laughed. "I'll be grateful not to finish last." I peered over her shoulder. "Is Eddie in?"

"Come in. He's upstairs. I'll go and get him for you."

The property was a typical house-share. Untidy. Kathy would have been right at home.

"He'll be down in a minute," Sasha said, when she came back down the stairs. "I guess I'll see you at the Levels then."

"Yeah. See you then. Thanks."

Eddie Lingard, a wizard, looked as though he'd only just woken up. His shorts were stained with what looked like strawberry jam, and his tee-shirt was inside out.

"I'm Eddie."

"Jill Gooder."

"What's this about?" he said, through a yawn.

"I'm a private investigator. I'm working for Beryl Christy."

His eyes widened. "Mrs Christy?"

"I believe you used to work at her bakery until recently?"

"That's right. In dispatch."

"Why were you dismissed?"

He shrugged. "You tell me."

"They must have given you a reason."

"Mrs Christy just said business was bad."

"No other reason?"

"Not as far as I know."

"Weren't you angry to get finished like that?"

"I was at first, but not now. It was just the boot up the backside I needed. I'm going to university to take a degree in English Lit. I start the month after next."

"Quite a change of direction."

"I should have gone to uni straight from school, but I was

in a relationship and we'd planned on getting married. I
needed to bring in a wage."

"What happened?"

"It didn't work out. She went off with the fish man."

"Who?" Was the Fish Man another kind of sup I hadn't
encountered before?

"The man who delivered the fish door-to-door. Chloe had
a thing for mackerel."

Somehow, I managed to keep a straight face and resist all
fish-related jokes. Well almost. "So you're stuck in this
plaice?" Come on. I'm allowed one.

"Until term begins."

"Do you still see Gary or any of the others from the
bakery?"

"No. I've been too busy preparing for my course. There's
a lot of reading to do."

"Costly business going to university. What with the books
and everything."

He picked at a nail, and bit his bottom lip. "I guess."

Something told me I'd struck a nerve, but even though I
pressed, I didn't get any more meaningful information out
of him.

"Good luck with the degree," I said, as I left.

I still couldn't work out why Eddie Lingard had been
dismissed. Beryl Christy had refused to elaborate, and he
had been far from forthcoming. And how on earth was he
funding his degree course?

"Your grandmother called in earlier," Mrs V said, as I
walked into the office.

"What did she want?"

"She left this." Mrs V handed me a white envelope which

had Kathy's name scrawled on the front. "She wants you to give it to your sister because she doesn't have her address. It's confirmation about her new job."

"Okay, thanks." I tucked it into my pocket. Maybe if I lost it, accidentally on purpose, Kathy would forget about the job. She had been very drunk the previous night.

"That cat is at it again." Mrs V gestured to my office.

"What's he done this time?"

"He's got one of the windows open."

"He hasn't got out again, has he?"

Some time back, Winky had made his escape through one of the windows when it had been left open by the man who'd come to repair my desk.

"No. He's sitting on the window ledge. It's freezing in there."

Sure enough, Winky was sitting out on the ledge, but that wasn't the whole story.

"What are you doing out there?" I said, as I made my way over to the window.

"What does it look like?"

"It looks like you're twiddling around with a phone."

"I thought *I* was meant to be the one with poor eye sight." He glared at me with his one good eye. "Does this look like a phone?"

He held it out towards me for closer inspection.

"I guess not. What is it?"

"It's a remote control, and for your information, I was not *twiddling around*. This is a precision operation."

"What is?"

Winky sighed a *'humans are so stupid'* sigh, and then pointed with his paw. "There!"

I stared out of the window. "What exactly am I supposed

to be looking at?"

He sighed an even deeper sigh. I'd obviously surpassed his expectations of human stupidity. "The helicopter!"

"Huh?"

"You know. It's like a plane but with—"

"I know what a helicopter is." Then I spotted it. A small blue helicopter was winging its way towards the building opposite, where Bella, the feline supermodel lived. In the distance I could see her sitting next to an open window.

"You have a helicopter," I said.

"Well spotted."

"How?"

"I feel the physics of helicopter flight are a little beyond you."

"I didn't mean how does it fly. I mean—err—I don't know what I mean."

"When you took me over to Bella's place, she and I decided that we should take our relationship to the next level."

"Which is?"

"Communicating via helicopter."

So, the Romeo and Juliet of the feline world had progressed from semaphore to remote control aircraft.

Across the way, Bella unclipped a small note, which had been attached to one of the helicopter's skis. She then scribbled her reply and attached it. Once Winky had seen her give the 'thumb's up', he manoeuvred the chopper back to our building, and landed it perfectly on the window ledge beside him. He tore off the paper, read it, and gave Bella a huge smile.

"What does it say?" I said, trying to get a look at the note.

"Never you mind. Just because you don't have a love life

doesn't mean you can share mine."

"I wasn't. I was just—can I have a go with the helicopter?"

"Do you have a pilot's licence?"

"It's only a toy."

He looked affronted. "Toy? I'll have you know this is a precision piece of aerodynamic engineering."

"So? Can I have a go?"

"Twenty pounds for fifteen minutes."

I gave Kathy a call. "Jill?" She sounded terrible.

"Where are you?" I said.

"On my way back home. I feel like death."

"It's your own fault."

"I knew I could rely on you for sympathy. What did Pete say when you told him I wasn't going home last night?"

"He sounded fine," I lied. "He said as long as you were having a good time, he didn't mind."

"Really?"

"No. He said you were a terrible mother and wife. And then he blamed me."

"That's good. If he thinks it's your fault, he might take it easy on me."

"It wasn't my fault. You and the twins went crazy. Talking of which, where are they?"

"They left just before I did. They said to tell you sorry about the microwave."

"Sorry? Microwave? What have they done to it?"

"Got to go. Pete's standing in the doorway. He doesn't look very happy."

"I hope he divorces you!"

She'd already hung up.

What had the twins done this time? It had taken me ages

to clear up after their last overnight stay. I prayed they hadn't set the microwave on fire—I'd never get rid of the smell.

After she'd hung up, it occurred to me that Kathy had never mentioned the job. Maybe she'd forgotten or thought it was a dream. Maybe, just maybe, if I forgot to deliver Grandma's letter, Kathy would never remember. Could I really do such a cruel thing to my sister? You bet your bottom dollar I could.

Chapter 16

I'd just stepped out of my office building onto the street when I felt someone tap me on the shoulder.

"Mr Armitage." I managed a half-hearted smile.

"You really must call me Gordon."

"I'm in rather a hurry, Gordon."

"I won't keep you. I was wondering if you'd had the chance to give any further thought to my proposal."

"I have."

"And?"

"And the answer is still no. You'll have to find alternative offices."

"I could make it worth your while."

"Look, Gordon. Like I told you before, my father started the business in these offices. I have a sentimental attachment—"

"There's no room for sentiment in business, Jill."

"The answer is still no." I took a step to one side.

"What's that?"

I followed his gaze up the side of the building.

"What?" I played dumb.

"That blue thing. It looks like—it looks like a small helicopter."

"I don't see anything."

"There! It's flying towards your office window. Look! You must see it now."

Just then, Winky's helicopter disappeared through the window.

"No, I didn't see anything. You must be imagining things. Got to rush."

Diamond Property Management was on the eighth floor. And the lift wasn't working.

"Hi." I managed while trying to catch my breath.

"How can I help you?" The receptionist, a vision in grey and pink, looked like she could take the seven flights of stairs without breaking sweat. I already hated her.

"I'm a private investigator." I was still gasping for air.

Patricia Daily—her name was on her badge—looked suitably unimpressed.

"I'm investigating the murder at Tregar Court. I'd like to see the records for the occupants of that building."

"Are you the police?"

"No, but I—"

"Then, I'm afraid you've had a wasted journey. The going is much easier on the way down."

"Is there someone else I could speak to? Your boss?"

"No. The exit is behind you." She pointed a finger in the direction from which I'd just staggered.

Not friendly. Not friendly at all.

Back on the stairs, I looked through the small glass pane in the door. Patricia Daily had a huge grin on her face. Not for long though. I'd got much better at the 'rain' spell since I'd started using it to water my bedding plants. It was so much easier than having to unravel the hosepipe and trail it all around the garden.

I manoeuvred the rain cloud as it moved closer and closer to the desk where an unsuspecting Ms Daily sat. When I was sure it was directly over her, I made it rain. And boy, did it rain. Within the space of no more than a few seconds, the grin had been well and truly washed off Ms Daily's face. Her cutesy bob now clung to her face. Her waterproof make-up had proved to be less than effective, and her clothes were saturated.

I dodged behind the door just before she came rushing out and flew down the stairs. After cancelling the spell, I walked past the reception desk and down a short corridor with doors on either side. I heard a handle turn, and immediately cast the 'invisible' spell. A middle-aged man, with a bad taste in ties, popped his head out of his office.

"Patricia? Are you alright?"

He'd obviously heard the receptionist's screams.

"Patricia?"

His concern didn't stretch as far as actually walking along the corridor to see if she was okay. Instead he just shook his head, and disappeared back into his office. It was good to know that the caring society was alive and well in Washbridge.

Fortunately for me, every door along the corridor had a small glass panel in it. Three of the rooms were occupied, but the last one I came to was empty. The name on the door was Samantha Brown. The computer on her desk was turned on, but as soon as I touched the mouse, a dialog box appeared asking for a password. I glanced around the desk just in case Samantha had conveniently left a Post-it note with the password on it. No such luck. Apart from the computer, the only thing on the desk was a photograph in a frame. The woman in the picture, who I assumed to be the absent Samantha Brown, was tall with unruly blonde hair. Next to her stood a much shorter man, and between them a pretty young girl about the same age as Lizzie. I tried a few obvious passwords, but none of them worked. I began to rifle through her drawers in search of any clues to the password when I heard footsteps in the corridor.

"Samantha?" It was the man who'd shown only fleeting concern for his receptionist. "I thought you were on holiday?"

The invisibility had worn off, but fortunately I managed to cast the 'doppelganger' spell just before he set foot in the door. From his point of view, I now looked and sounded like his colleague.

"We're leaving later today," I said. "There were a few things I needed to finish."

"Really?" The puzzled look on his face told me that Samantha Brown was not normally the kind of person who'd show up to work during her vacation.

"I had to call in town to buy a new case anyway," I said.

"I thought you were going hiking?"

Whoops. She didn't look like the hiking type. I'd had her down as a sun worshipper who preferred to laze beside the pool.

"Yeah, that's what I meant," I stuttered. "A rucksack. The strap on the old one broke last night."

"Oh, okay. Well enjoy your holiday."

I waited until I heard his door close, and then resumed my search of the desk. Sure enough, in the bottom drawer was an old diary. On the inside back cover was an eight digit sequence of characters and letters. It was worth a try. Bingo!

Once I'd logged on, I soon found the menu for the property management system. From there, it was remarkably easy to bring up all of the records for Tregar Court—everything from the resident's personal details through to their payment record. As I'd suspected, Jason Allan wasn't paying the rent on his apartment. But I now knew who was.

I managed to get out of the office and back to the stairs without anyone seeing me. I bumped into Patricia Daily on the sixth floor.

"Is it raining out?" I said, and almost managed to keep a straight face.

She mumbled something about the sprinkler system as she pushed past me.

I rushed straight over to Tregar Court.

"Can I come in?" I said.

"I'm busy." Jason Allan had the door on a chain again.

"Please. This won't take a minute."

He sighed, but undid the chain and pulled open the door.

"I've told you everything I know," he said, once we were in the kitchen.

"How do you manage to pay the rent on this place, Jason?"

He shrugged, and then took a drink from a milk carton. The white moustache was a little off-putting, but I persevered.

"You don't pay it, do you?"

He shrugged again, finished the milk, and dumped the carton into an already overflowing bin. "What's it got to do with you?"

"I'm trying to find out who murdered the man in the lift."

"What's that got to do with my rent?"

"The man on the third floor; the man who was murdered in the lift—he was the one paying your rent. Now would you like to explain to me why he would do that?"

Jason grabbed a hold of the breakfast bar, and for a moment I thought his legs were going to give way.

"What are you talking about?" All the blood had drained

from his face.

"The man who was murdered, Alan Dennis, had been paying your rent ever since you moved in. Are you going to deny that?"

He didn't deny it. He didn't speak at all. Instead he struggled onto one of the stools next to the breakfast bar. He was as white as a sheet.

"Why would he do that?" His voice was barely audible.

"I think you already know."

"I have no idea!" He shouted, having found his voice again. "I don't understand."

"You might as well tell me. The police will find out soon enough and they —"

"I've already told you. I didn't know."

"You weren't even a tiny bit curious who was paying it?"

"Of course I was, but the lawyer who contacted me about moving to Tregar said that it was a condition of the tenancy that I could never know who made the payments."

"I don't believe you."

"It's true."

"You seriously expect me to believe that you didn't know it was your father who was paying your rent?"

He stared at me for the longest moment. "Who?"

"Your father."

"But you said it was the man on the third floor. The man who was murdered."

"Alan Dennis *was* your father. Don't pretend you didn't know."

He didn't have to. He didn't have to say a word. No one could have put on that kind of performance. Jason Allan could barely speak, and he looked ill.

I hung around in the hope that he might recover enough for me to ask him some more questions, but it soon became obvious that wasn't going to happen any time soon. He was in an almost catatonic state. After twenty minutes, I let myself out.

I asked for Jack Maxwell at the front desk of the police station. Ten minutes later, Sushi and her curly blonde hair appeared.

"I want to speak to Jack."

"Come with me." She led me to the familiar interview room.

"I need a word with Jack," I said again once we were alone.

"I've told you. I'm now your contact. Anything you have to say or report must come through me."

"It's about the Tregar case."

"What about it?"

"I'd prefer to speak to—"

"Jill." Jack Maxwell walked into the room. "Someone said you were here."

"I did ask for you."

He glanced at Sushi who shrugged. "I've told Ms Gooder that I'm her point of contact now, but she can't seem to get that through her thick head."

For the briefest of moments, I thought I saw a look of anger on Maxwell's face, but then it was gone.

"Susan is now on my team," he said. "She should be able to help you with anything you need."

"Really?" I took two steps closer to him. "Because from where I'm standing, it looks like she's just stonewalling me. I thought we'd agreed—"

Sushi stepped in between me and Maxwell, like a she-cat claiming her mate. "I've already told Ms Gooder that we don't need her trampling all over police business."

Maxwell glanced at Sushi and then at me.

"Susan. Would you mind leaving me and Ms Gooder alone for a few minutes?"

"But, Jack—" she began.

"Please. Just for a few minutes."

She stared at him for a moment, and then glared at me. "Fine. I'll be in the office."

"Thanks, Susan," Maxwell said.

"Thanks, Susan," I mocked, once she was out of the door.

"What was that all about?" he said.

"Your stupid girlfriend is giving me grief. I thought we'd agreed we'd try to work together."

"We did."

"Then why, when I'm trying to bring you information, do you send out Sushi to block me?"

He laughed. "Sushi?"

"The woman is a nightmare."

"Susan is a first rate detective."

"Who has the hots for you."

"Don't be ridiculous. Ours is a purely professional relationship."

"Tell me again. How did you make detective? If you can't see that she wants to get into your pants, then—"

"That's enough. What information did you want to give to me?"

I told Maxwell that I'd discovered the victim was Jason Allan's father. I'd recognised him in the photograph which Jason's sister had shown me. I also told Maxwell about the rent payments.

"And Jason Allan claims he didn't know?"

"I believe him. I saw the look on his face when I told him the murdered man was his father. He wasn't lying."

"Okay." Maxwell checked his watch. "I have to get going, but thanks for bringing this to me."

"I'm not going to keep doing this if Sushi sticks her oar in every time."

"I'll have a word with Susan."

"Make it two: *butt* and *out!*"

Chapter 17

"Morning," I said, as I walked into Cuppy C.

"Morning." Amber smiled nervously. "If it's about the microwave. It was Pearl's fault."

"It wasn't my fault." Pearl had seen me arrive, and had walked through from the cake counter. "You were the one who wanted bread for a sandwich!"

"You forgot it was in there!"

"I wasn't the one who wanted a sandwich."

"Girls, girls! Forget about it. It's all sorted now."

I hadn't been quite so relaxed about it when I'd got home to discover that my kitchen smelled of charcoal. The twins had put bread from my freezer in the microwave to thaw it, but had then forgotten all about it. It had taken two cans of air freshener to get rid of the smell, and I'd had to throw out the old microwave. I might have been more annoyed, but it had been on its last legs anyway.

"We're sorry about that other thing too." Pearl handed me the coffee. "At the club."

"Yeah, we're really sorry." Amber refused my payment. "This is on the house. It's the least we can do."

The three of us sat at our usual window table. "It's no excuse," Amber said. "But we were a little drunk."

"No kidding." I laughed. "Still, it was your birthday."

"Even so, we shouldn't have used magic like that. We could be in real trouble if anyone ever finds out."

"They won't hear it from me, and I don't think you have to worry about the other people in the club. Most of them were drunk too. By the next morning, they probably thought it had all been some drunken dream."

Cuppy C was quieter than usual. The only other

customers were two vampires who were tucking into chocolate muffins.

"It's quiet in here this morning," I remarked.

"It was busier earlier," Pearl said. "The morning rush is over now. It'll pick up again in an hour or two."

"It will if you haven't scared them all off." Amber glared at her sister.

"Don't start that again!" Pearl glared back.

Here we go again.

"*She* tried to poison the customers." Amber pointed an accusing finger at Pearl.

"Don't listen to her. There was nothing wrong with those cupcakes."

Amber began to laugh hysterically. "Nothing wrong? Apart from the shape, colour and taste you mean?" She took her phone out of her pocket, pulled up an image, and handed the phone to me. "Have you ever seen anything quite like that?"

I hadn't. If it was a cupcake, it was like none I'd ever seen before. It was kind of cube shaped and sort of dark blue with grey specks.

"See what I mean?" Amber wiped tears of laughter from her eyes. "And it tasted like—"

"At least I tried." Pearl's face was red with rage. "What do you ever do?"

"Not poison the customers, for a start."

"I didn't poison anyone."

"Jimmy Logan bought one. I haven't seen him since. Mrs Perry bought one. I haven't seen her since either."

"That's just a coincidence," Pearl said, with very little conviction.

"How come you baked cakes for the shop? I thought you

always bought them in."

Pearl was still looking daggers at her sister. "With the problem we're having with Christy's, I thought it would be better if we weren't so dependent on outside suppliers. I thought if we could bake our own—"

"That you could kill off all our customers!" Amber laughed and then ducked just in time to avoid the muffin which Pearl had launched at her head. *My* muffin.

"Sorry, Jill. I'll get you another one," Pearl said. "She just makes me so angry."

"It's okay. I probably shouldn't have ordered it anyway." I took hold of their hands. "Look you two. This business will only succeed if you work together."

"It's her!" Pearl said.

"I'm not the one poisoning the customers!"

"Enough! One more word and I'll tell everyone what happened in the club."

Suddenly they were both focussed on me.

"You wouldn't?"

"You promised."

"If you don't stop all this silly squabbling and start to work together, I will tell. Understand?"

They both nodded.

"Do you promise?"

They were still glaring at one another, but nodded.

"I need to hear you say it. Do you promise?"

"I promise."

"Me too."

"Good. That's settled then."

I brought the twins up-to-date on my investigation into the Christy Bakery. Not that there was much to tell. My only lead was Eddie Lingard. Something about his dismissal still didn't ring true.

"Hello you two!" a male voice from behind me said.

The look of horror on the twins' faces should have tipped me off, but I didn't recognise the voice at first.

"Miles?" Amber said.

"Miles?" Pearl echoed.

"Hello, Miles." I was the only one to greet him with a smile. "You probably don't remember me. We met outside the school reunion."

"Err — oh yes."

He obviously had no idea who I was, and had eyes only for the twins.

"I thought I'd find you here," he said. "It's a pity you both had to rush off the other night."

"That *was* a pity," I said, as I stood up. "I have to be going. Miles, why don't you take my seat. I'm sure you and the girls have *lots* to catch up on."

Amber and Pearl glared at me. If looks could kill.

I was still sniggering to myself five minutes after leaving Cuppy C. The look on the twins' faces when they saw Miles had been priceless.

"What are you looking so pleased with yourself about?"

The sound of her voice instantly pulled me out of my good mood.

"Grandma? I didn't see you there."

"Hardly surprising if you walk around with your head in the clouds. What's amusing you?"

"Oh, nothing."

"Do you usually laugh at nothing?"

"All the time."

"Sometimes I worry about you, young lady."

Somehow I doubted that.

"I trust you are putting in plenty of practice for the Levels?"

"Every spare minute."

"My reputation is at stake. I won't be pleased if you let me down."

"I'll do my best."

"Hmm. I suppose that will have to do."

"I'd better make tracks."

"Wait. You're supposed to be a private investigator aren't you?"

"I'm not *supposed to be*. I *am*."

"Well then. What's wrong with Lucy?"

"What do you mean?"

"She doesn't seem herself. I'm not sure what it is. Like this morning, I insulted her porridge, and she just let it go. Normally, she'd have given as good as she got."

I knew what Grandma meant. Aunt Lucy had seemed a little subdued recently, and I thought I knew why, but I wasn't about to tell Grandma.

"So, it's Fester," Grandma said.

When would I learn she could read my mind at will?

"His name is Lester."

"Fester, that's what I said. Has he done something to upset her? If he has, I'll turn him into the rat he is."

"No! No need for that. I don't think he's done anything, he just hasn't been around. I'm not sure even Aunt Lucy knows why."

"Or a cockroach."

"You mustn't turn him into anything. At least not until we know what's going on."

"Well then, Miss Investigator, you'd better go do some investigating. And if you find out he's been messing Lucy around, just you let me know. Got it?"

"Aye, aye, captain."

She gave me a look.

"I mean. Yes, Grandma. I'll get straight on it."

Well maybe not *straight* on it. First I had an appointment with Annie Christy, the bakery owner's daughter. She'd called me the day before to ask if I'd meet with her away from the bakery, and had specifically requested that I didn't mention our meeting to her mother.

We met at 'In a Jam', a small tea room close to the bakery. The tea room, which was obviously a competitor of Cuppy C, was even quieter than the twins' shop. Annie Christy and I were the only customers. I'd met Annie before at her mother's house, but only briefly. She had the air of a young professional.

"I work for SupAid," she said. "It's a charity. We provide financial and other aid to sups that have lost their powers."

"Does that happen?"

"Not often, fortunately, but yes. Witches can lose their magical powers. Werewolves can lose the power to transform into wolves."

"What about vampires?"

"They can lose their teeth."

I must have looked puzzled because she laughed.

"I'm joking. With vampires, the issue is usually that they can no longer get the nutrients they need from blood. Whatever the problem, SupAid steps in to help."

"And what's your role?"

"I'm their official spokesperson. So mainly PR."

I took a bite of my blueberry muffin. What? Why

shouldn't I have another? The one I had in Cuppy C had been thrown across the shop after I'd taken only one bite out of it. "This tastes like one of your mother's."

Annie smiled. "She'd be pleased you can tell. Yes, Mum's bakery supplies most of the cake shops and tea rooms in this part of Candlefield."

"It's delicious," I said through a mouthful of muffin. "Why did you want to see me?"

"I'm a little worried about the recent incidents. I wondered how your investigation was coming along."

"Why not ask your mother?"

"I've tried, but she gets awfully upset every time the subject is raised."

"I haven't made much progress to be honest, but there are still a few leads I need to follow up on."

"My main concern is that it may affect the sale of the business."

"It's for sale?"

"Didn't Mum tell you? I've already found a potential buyer, but I'm worried the recent incidents might put him off."

"Your mother never mentioned she was intending to sell the bakery."

"She isn't getting any younger, and I'm worried that she'll work herself into an early grave before she has a chance to enjoy her retirement. That's why I persuaded her to sell."

"I see."

I think I managed to satisfy Annie that I was doing all I could to get to the bottom of the damaged cakes mystery, and I promised to keep her, as well as her mother, updated on my investigation. I came away with the impression that she was genuinely concerned for her mother's well-being, but I was also a little curious as to why Beryl Christy had never once mentioned the potential sale.

Back in Washbridge, I was about to cross the road to my offices when I spotted Gordon Armitage standing outside the building next door. He checked his watch and looked left and right along the street as though he was waiting for someone.

The light at the crossing turned green just as I spotted Zak Whiteside, the landlord of my building. I'd only met with him once when I took over the lease after my father's death. Once seen, never forgotten, Zak Whiteside had the worst fitting toupee I'd ever seen. I could only assume that he'd bought it second-hand, and that it had originally been made for a man with a head three sizes smaller than his. It looked more like a cap resting on the top of his head. Still, it had great comedic value. Armitage had obviously been waiting for the landlord because he greeted him with a warm smile and a firm handshake. Even from this distance, I noticed Armitage's gaze drift up to Zak's toupee. Credit to Armitage, he somehow managed to keep a straight face.

I crossed the road, and stood outside the door to my offices. Armitage and Zak Whiteside were walking my way, and it didn't take a genius to guess why.

Chapter 18

I ran up the stairs as fast as my legs would carry me, and yelled, "Quick!"

Poor old Mrs V almost jumped out of her skin. "What's wrong?"

"You need to take down this line now."

"But, I've nowhere else to put the socks."

"Sorry, but the landlord is on his way up. He's not going to be very impressed if he gets strangled by a washing line full of socks as soon as he walks through the door."

"Okay." Mrs V was on her feet. "I'm on it."

"Hey, what are you doing?" Winky yelled at me when I snatched the remote control from him. "The helicopter will crash."

"Tough!" I slammed the window closed, grabbed Winky and pushed him under the leather sofa. "Stay there and don't move!"

"Who do you think you are?" Winky was already back out from under the sofa. "Give me the remote back!"

This was never going to work. The chances of Winky staying hidden were less than zero.

I heard voices in the outer office.

Mrs V opened the door. Standing behind her were Gordon Armitage and Zak Whiteside.

"Hello, gentlemen." I had to force myself not to look at Zak's toupee. "To what do I owe this unexpected pleasure?"

Zak led Armitage inside my office. "Nice to see you again, Jill. You know Gordon Armitage?"

"Yes, we've met."

"Mr Armitage has made a report which I felt I had to investigate. I'm sure you understand."

"What kind of report?" As if I didn't know.

"Mr Armitage says that you are keeping a cat in the office."

"A cat?" I looked suitably shocked. "But, surely animals aren't allowed?"

I glanced at Armitage whose eyes were darting left and right in an attempt to spot Winky.

Meanwhile, the cat in question was scratching the back of my legs. I'd cast the 'hide' spell on him just before the two men walked into my office, so they couldn't see him. He was one angry cat, not least because his precious helicopter had almost certainly plunged to its destruction. I shook my leg to knock him off.

"Are you okay?" Zak said when he saw my leg twitch.

"Fine. Just a bit of cramp."

Armitage was still surveying the room, trying to find any trace of the cat. Fortunately, Winky's bowls were out of sight in the bottom drawer of my desk.

"He's only got one eye," Armitage said.

"Who has?" Zak looked confused.

"Her cat. The ugly brute has only got one eye."

I felt Winky flinch at the words 'ugly brute'. If he launched an attack on Armitage, it would be game over. Fortunately, or unfortunately, depending on how you looked at it, he was still way more annoyed with me, so he continued to claw at my leg.

"Are you sure you're alright, Jill?" Zak asked. "You look in some discomfort."

"I'm fine thanks. I just had a little too much curry last night, I think."

That seemed to have the desired effect.

"I think we're done here." Zak moved back to the door.

"She has a cat," Armitage protested. "I saw him with my own eyes."

"Why would I keep a cat in the office?" I smiled sweetly at Armitage.

"Thanks again for your time." Zak led the way out.

Armitage turned to me. "This isn't over."

I waited until I'd heard them leave, and then reversed the 'hide' spell. Winky was attached to my legs with his claws.

"Get off!" I shook him off, sending him sliding across the floor. "Look what you've done!" I pointed to the scratch marks on the back of my legs. "I could have you arrested and thrown in cat jail for that."

"Never mind your legs. What about my helicopter. Give me the remote."

I threw the control at his head, but somehow he managed to catch it. He had good hands for a cat. Moments later he'd opened the window and was surveying the road for signs of wreckage.

"Lucky for you," he said.

"I don't feel very lucky," I said, as I patted my poor legs with a tissue.

"Bella managed to grab the chopper before it crash landed."

"I'm so very relieved."

"You should be. You would have had to buy me a new one if it had crashed."

I wasn't sure who I should be more angry with. Winky for being a psycho or Armitage for trying to get me thrown out of my offices. I settled on Armitage—he didn't have such sharp claws. I'd get my own back on Mr Gordon Armitage.

I was still dabbing blood from the scratches on my legs when Mrs V came back into my office. Or at least, I assumed it was Mrs V, because I had my back to the door.

"What happened to your legs?" Jack Maxwell said.

I hurriedly turned around and threw the bloody tissue into the waste basket.

"The cat mistook me for his scratching post." I pointed to Winky.

"*He* did that? That animal is a psycho. Why don't you get rid of him?"

"He's quite sweet really." Who was I kidding?

"What's he doing anyway?"

I glanced across at Winky. Oh bum, I'd forgotten he still had the remote control.

"Oh that? It's—err—it's just a cat toy I picked up at the market."

"It looks like some kind of remote control."

"Does it? Oh, yeah. I hadn't noticed."

I just hoped that Maxwell wouldn't see the helicopter. How was I meant to explain that away?

"What brings you here, Detective?"

"There's news on the Tregar Court murder. I was passing by anyway, and thought you'd want to know."

"Thanks, but are you sure that Sushi won't mind?"

He gave me a cutting look.

"Sorry, she just winds me up."

"Susan is a first class detective. She'll be an asset to the Washbridge force."

Yawn. "If you say so."

"I wanted to let you know that Jason Allan has been found dead. Suicide."

That was the last thing I'd expected. Sure, he'd been in shock when I'd told him about Alan Dennis, but I never dreamed he would kill himself.

"Are you sure it was suicide?"

"Pretty much. The handwriting on the note is definitely his."

"Poor guy."

"That's not all. In his suicide note he confessed to murdering Alan Dennis. He also made a point of saying that he'd had no idea the man was his father or even that he was paying his rent."

"Why did Jason kill him? It's not as though he knew he was his father."

"Who says he didn't know? We only have Allan's word for that."

"I saw his reaction when I told him. He was in complete shock. There's no way he knew before."

"Either way, he made a full confession."

"But, why wasn't the murder captured on tape?"

"We may never know. Anyway, I just wanted to bring you up to speed. I assume you'll let your client know."

"Yeah, thanks. And thank Sushi for me."

Maxwell shook his head. "You really should cut Susan some slack. You two are more similar than you might like to think."

Way to insult someone.

It was like Piccadilly Circus in my office. No sooner had Maxwell left, than Kathy walked in.

"I passed Jacky Boy on the stairs." She had a stupid grin on her face. "You two an item again?"

"We were never an item. We went out a couple of times — that's all."

"I'll believe you, thousands wouldn't. What did he want?"

"Nothing. Just work stuff."

"How come his new girlfriend wasn't with him?"

"She's not his girlfriend." I jumped in much too quickly.

"Okay. Keep your hair on. Why do you care if you're not interested in him?"

"I don't. I was just saying — never mind — what brings you here? Do you need another favour?"

"Charming. Anyone would think the only time I come to see my sister is to ask a favour."

"That's because it is. What is it this time?"

"It just so happens you're wrong. I came because I have a bone to pick with you."

"What did I do?"

"I believe you have something for me."

I shook my head. I had no idea what she was talking about.

"Something your grandmother asked you to give to me?"

Whoops. Busted. "Oh yeah. I totally forgot."

"Liar. You just don't want me to work at her shop."

"I did you a favour. You'd have hated working there. That woman can be a slave driver."

"Is that what you think of me?" Grandma walked through from the outer office.

"Grandma?" I glared at Kathy who was enjoying my discomfort way too much. "You didn't tell me that Grandma was with you."

"It must have slipped my mind just like you forgot to give

me her note."

"I'm pleased to say that your sister has accepted my job offer, "Grandma said. "We both wanted to give you the good news."

Yay! "That's—err—great."

"I start next week."

Kathy was obviously thrilled—we'd see how long that lasted. Poor, delusional fool.

"What's that buzzing noise?" Grandma asked.

I glanced at the window and saw the helicopter on its final approach.

"Must be workmen in the street," I lied.

"What's the cat doing?" Kathy stared at Winky who was pressing the lever on his remote control.

"That's his new toy."

"What is it?"

"I'm not sure. I think it's meant to look like a phone or something."

"It looks more like the remote control that Mikey has for his car."

"Really? Do you think so?"

"Aren't cat toys usually mice or fish?"

"I thought he might like something different." I grabbed Winky and slammed the window shut. "Now, I have to get going. I have an appointment." I herded Kathy and Grandma out of the office, down the stairs and outside. Moments later there was a crash a few yards away—just down the street from where we were standing.

"What was that?" Kathy yelled.

Grandma surveyed the tangle of metal and plastic on the ground. "It looks like some kind of toy helicopter."

Beryl Christy wasn't in her office, but then I deliberately hadn't called ahead. Her secretary, Polly Waites, would have made a matching bookend with Mrs V. Except of course that Polly didn't spend all day knitting.

She had no idea when Mrs Christy would be back, but she'd been told that I should be given access to any information I needed.

"Where are the HR and payroll records kept?" I asked.

"I look after all of that."

"Could I see the HR record for Eddie Lingard?"

"I'm sorry, but Eddie's details are no longer on the system."

"Is it usual to remove an employee's records when they leave?"

"No, but Mrs Christy specifically asked for Eddie's to be deleted."

"I see. What about his payroll details? Did those get deleted too?"

"No, because he's still being paid."

"How come?"

"I'm not really sure. Mrs Christy said to leave him on the payroll for now."

"Right. Thank you for your help."

Eddie Lingard had been dismissed for reasons unknown. Reasons which Mrs Christy refused to discuss. And yet, he was still being paid by the company who had dismissed him. I could think of only one explanation.

Chapter 19

Yay for garden parties! Don't try to tell me that anyone actually enjoys them. What? *You* do? You freak!

Still, I had to admit that as garden parties go, this one was a cut above the average. As well as the usual cake, plant and tombola stalls organised by the locals, Colonel Briggs had brought in a number of fairground stalls and rides. I hadn't expected there to be so many people there, but then it was a beautiful, sunny day.

"You could at least try to look as though you're enjoying yourself," Kathy said.

"I am." I gave her my cheesiest grin. "Look!"

"Sometimes you're just plain weird," she said. "Have you seen Pete?"

"The last time I saw him he was complaining about the mess that the crowds were making of the lawns. Where are the kids?"

"They probably went home crying because their Auntie Jill was ignoring them."

"Don't be horrible. I wasn't ignoring them, it's just that the grass is damp, and my heels keep getting stuck."

"It might have helped if you'd worn sensible shoes. What were you thinking?"

Kathy was right—as usual. What had I been thinking? Heels and garden parties don't mix. "So where are the kids?"

"They're with Kylie's mum."

"Who's Kylie?"

"One of Lizzie's friends. The last time I saw them they were headed for the carousel. Why don't you go look for them?"

I glanced at my shoes. Oh well, it was time to take one for the cause.

I was making my way gingerly across the lawn when I heard a familiar voice.

"Jill, glad you could make it."

"Colonel, hi."

I'd worked on a case for Colonel Briggs recently. After retiring from the military, he'd taken the reins of a dog rescue charity. He'd come to me when he'd suspected that one of the charity's supporters had been murdered because she'd intended bequeathing money to Washbridge Dog Rescue. My investigations had revealed it had been a little more complicated than that, but everything had worked out okay in the end, and the charity had received a substantial donation from one of the deceased's children. Better still, the colonel had given Kathy's husband, Peter, a job looking after his estate's grounds and gardens.

"Are you okay?" the colonel asked. "It looked like you were limping."

"I'm fine. It's just—" I gestured to my shoes.

"I have some wellingtons you can borrow. They may be a little on the large side."

One glance at the colonel's feet told me they'd be more than a *little* on the large side. "Thanks, I'll be okay."

"What do you think to all this?" He looked around. "Are you enjoying yourself?"

"Err—yeah. I love garden parties." Hypocrite? Who, me? "I was just telling Kathy how much I was enjoying myself."

"I'm afraid that Peter may not share your enthusiasm.

He's worried what it might do to the lawns."

"He takes his job very seriously."

"I can't thank you enough for recommending him to me. He's doing a sterling job. I was just headed for the refreshments tent. Will you join me?"

"Maybe later. I have to find my nephew and niece."

"Okay, well enjoy yourself."

Standing in one spot for any length of time was not a good idea—my heels were now wedged deep into the soft ground. After much swaying back and forth, I eventually managed to dislodge them, and continue on my stumbling way.

"Auntie Jill!" Lizzie shouted. "Where have you been?"

"Why are you walking funny?" Mikey threw his arms around me. "Have you hurt your foot?"

"No, Mikey, I just chose the wrong shoes."

The woman who'd been standing with them, who I took to be Kylie's mum, glanced down at my feet.

"Hi," I said, trying to keep my balance. "I'm Kathy's sister."

"Right." She smiled. "Kathy has told me all about you."

She had? What did that mean exactly? Nothing good, I'd wager.

"You're a private investigator aren't you? How exciting."

"Not as much as you might think."

"Still. You must see some things. What are you working on now? Anything gruesome?"

That was my cue to leave.

"Sorry, I promised Kathy I'd take these two home. Thanks for looking after them. Come on kids!"

I grabbed Lizzie and Mikey by the hand, and dragged them behind the candy floss stall.

"I don't want to go home!" Lizzie stamped her feet.

"It's not time yet!" Mikey protested.

"It's okay. We're not going home."

"But you said—"

"It was just a joke. I was playing a trick on Kylie's mum." I checked behind me to make sure she hadn't followed us—the coast was clear. "So, what do you two want to do?"

"Win a bear!" Lizzie screamed. Why can't kids speak at a normal volume?

"I want to win a bee! A giant bee!" Mikey yelled.

"Where can we win those?" I asked.

"Well," Lizzie said, quite serious now. "To win a bear you have to knock a coconut down. To win a giant bee—which are stupid—"

"Giant bees are not stupid," Mikey protested.

"Yes they are. Bees aren't supposed to be giant. They're supposed to be tiny."

"You have to throw a hoop over a block of wood," Mikey said.

"It's very hard." Lizzie sighed. "I've had three goes, and I couldn't even hit the coconut."

"That's because you're a rubbish thrower," Mikey said. "I nearly got the hoop over the block."

"No you didn't!"

"I did!"

"You didn't!"

"Okay! Okay! Let's go and take a look at the stalls. Maybe I can win something for you."

The garden party was divided into two distinct areas. On one side were all the stalls run by locals. On the other side were the fairground stalls and rides. Peter had told me that Colonel Briggs had reached an agreement with the fairground owner that the stalls and rides would be provided to him free of charge, but that all takings would be theirs.

The grey haired man at the coconut stall had a face which was more like a coconut than the coconuts themselves.

"How much is it?" I enquired.

He pointed to the board on the far side of the stall: *three balls for one pound*.

I handed over a pound coin, and he dropped three red balls on the counter in front of me. My first attempt missed by a foot.

"I told you girls can't throw," Mikey said to his sister.

Cheek! I'd show him.

My second attempt caught the coconut square on, but it didn't budge.

I put everything I had behind my final attempt. That too hit the coconut full on, but still it didn't budge.

"Unlucky," coconut-face said.

Lizzie looked so sad, it was heartbreaking.

"Come and try the hoops." Mikey grabbed my hand and dragged me over to the hoopla stall. Lizzie followed.

"Hello, darling!" A young man with floppy blond hair greeted me. "Where's your boyfriend? You lost him?"

"Three hoops please." I handed him a pound coin.

"Three hoops for the prettiest girl here today."

This guy was about as subtle as a sledge hammer, but judging by the crowd of young girls hanging around the stall, his approach was having some success. Which was more than I had with any of the three hoops. All three found their target, but none of them covered the block.

"Unlucky, darling. Why don't you have another go?"

I declined. Something just didn't smell right to me.

"Sorry kids. Looks like we're out of luck. Let's go and find your mum."

Kathy had tomato sauce all over her top lip from the foot long hot-dog she was devouring.

"What have you done now?" she asked me through a mouthful of bread and sausage.

"What do you mean?"

She pointed to the kids who both looked on the verge of tears.

"I haven't done anything. They wanted me to try and win them a prize on the coconut shy and hoopla, but I didn't manage it." I stepped closer so I could whisper. "I think they're rigged."

"Never mind kids." She crouched down. "Why don't I buy you both some candy floss?"

"Can I have a toffee apple instead?" Mikey said.

"Of course you can."

Kathy and the kids disappeared in the direction of the candy floss stall. I made an excuse, and made my way back to the coconut shy. Standing to one side, I watched a procession of punters take turns at trying to dislodge the fruits. Some of them were simply hopeless, and missed the coconuts entirely. Others managed to find their mark, but with nowhere near enough power to have any effect. But, at least three different men hit the coconuts with enough power that the fruit should have been dislodged. Coconut-face dismissed their complaints as sour grapes. Meanwhile he continued to rake in the cash without once having to give out a prize. Something definitely wasn't right.

I handed coconut-face my payment in return for another

three balls. I cast the 'power' spell just before I took my first throw. My first attempt missed by inches, and crashed into the back wall with such force that the whole stall reverberated. My second attempt caught the coconut dead centre, and knocked it off the post and into the back wall. Coconut face stared in disbelief—first at the coconut, and then at me. My final throw hit another coconut full on—this time the fruit smashed into a thousand pieces.

"I'll have two of those bears, please." I pointed to the large orange bears on the top shelf at the side of the stall.

Coconut-face looked shell shocked, but recovered in time to say. "One prize per person only." He pointed to the small print on the bottom of the price board.

"Just give me one then."

With the bear tucked under my arm, I made my way over to the hoopla. Here again, I watched punter after punter attempt to get a hoop over a block of wood. Not once did anyone manage it. I was absolutely sure that it was impossible despite the fact that the stall holder regularly demonstrated that it could be done. I didn't know how he was doing it, but my best guess was that the ring he used was marginally larger than those which he handed to the punters.

I hadn't actually used the 'smaller' spell before although I had memorised it. Similar to the 'shrink' spell, it would allow me to reduce the size of an object. The blond guy was still flirting outrageously as I paid for another three hoops. Just like the coconut shy, this stall also had a 'one prize per person' rule written in text so small it was practically invisible. I threw the first hoop which only managed to clip the block. My second attempt landed on the block, but didn't completely cover it. Before I threw the final hoop, I chose the block I intended to aim for, cast the 'smaller' spell and then tossed the hoop. My aim was true, and this time the hoop slipped easily over the block.

Blond guy was so busy flirting with every female who came within ten yards of the stall that he didn't even notice I'd won.

"Excuse me," I said.

"What is it, darling?"

"I've won."

He looked confused for a few seconds until I pointed at the hoop. Now, he looked even more confused. The expression on his face confirmed what I'd suspected: it shouldn't have been possible for me to win.

"I'll have one of those giant bees, please."

"But—err—?"

"I'll have a bee please." If only his name had been Bob, my day would have been complete.

Blond guy kept glancing back at my winning hoop as he handed me the giant bee.

"Thanks, *bee* seeing you." What? Come on, you knew that was coming.

The kids' faces lit up as soon as they saw me hobbling towards them.

"Thanks, Auntie Jill!" Mikey grabbed the giant bee.

"Thanks!" Lizzie hugged the bear.

Kathy looked at me with a puzzled expression. "How?" She mouthed the word.

"Girl's got skillz."

Chapter 20

I wasn't looking forward to going to the office. I hadn't been back there since the incident with the helicopter. Something told me that I wouldn't be Winky's favourite person.

"Morning, Mrs V." I was surprised to see that she hadn't put the line of socks back up.

"Morning, Jill. How did it go with the landlord?"

"I think we're okay for now, but I wouldn't trust Armitage as far as I could throw him. I don't think he's going to give up just yet."

"That's what I thought too. I decided it would be better not to put up the sock line again until this has all blown over."

"I think that's wise. What time is Jackie Langford coming in?"

"She should be here any time now."

Jackie Langford had contacted me after the news of Jason Allan's suicide and confession had broken in the news. I wasn't sure yet what I was going to tell her. As far as the police were concerned, the Alan Dennis case was now cut and dried. I still had some reservations, not least the CCTV from the lift.

Oh well, I couldn't put it off any longer. Time to face the wrath of Winky.

"I need milk," Winky called from the window sill. The window was closed and he had the little flags in his paws.

"Sure." I grabbed the milk carton from the fridge and poured some into his dish.

"Thanks." He put down the flags, jumped down from the window, and began to lap up the milk.

I didn't trust him. This was obviously some ploy to catch me off guard. The moment I thought he'd forgiven me, he'd attack. "I see you're using the flags again."

He ignored me until he'd lapped up the last of the milk, and then said, "Turns out you did me a favour. Bella thought the helicopter was a little too impersonal. She's decided semaphore is more romantic after all."

"So, you and I are okay?" I said.

"I guess so."

"Good." I checked my watch. "Look, I have a client due in a few minutes. Do you think you could hold off on the semaphore until she's gone?"

"What's it worth?"

"Salmon."

"Red?"

"Pink."

"Okay. Deal."

Jackie Langford arrived on time. "Thanks for seeing me at such short notice."

"No problem. Have a seat."

She looked around the office. "Where's that handsome cat of yours?"

Before I could answer, Winky strutted out from under the sofa.

"You are a handsome boy." She stroked him; Winky lapped up the attention. "I could take you home with me." If only she meant it.

I had to raise my voice to be heard over Winky's purring. "How can I help?"

Jackie Langford gave Winky one final tickle under the chin, and then turned her attention back to me.

"The newspapers say that the young man who murdered Alan was his son. Is that true?"

"Yes. Apparently, Alan had been paying his son's rent for some time. I spoke to Jason Allan. He said he had no idea that Alan was his father, and hadn't known who was making the payments."

"Did you believe him?"

"Yes. Either he was an incredible actor or he genuinely didn't have a clue."

"Why did he murder Alan?"

"No one knows the motive for the murder. The police think Jason may have committed suicide once he realised it was his father he had killed."

"What do you think?"

"I don't know what to think. I do believe that Jason didn't know Alan was his father or about the payments. The CCTV still bothers me though."

"Will you stay on the case?"

"That's up to you. I don't want to keep running up charges on a case which the police consider to be closed unless you specifically want me to."

"I think there's more to it. I'd like you to stick with it for a little longer at least."

"I'll be happy to. Is there anything more you can tell me about Alan? Anything at all?"

"He didn't talk much about his life. I knew he'd been in at least one serious long term relationship, but that had broken down. Money problems, I believe."

"And he never mentioned having a son?"

"No, never."

Sometimes the old ways are the best. My father hated

computers, and preferred to scribble notes and diagrams onto an A4 pad. He said it helped him to see the big picture — to see how the different elements of a case came together. Well, if it was good enough for Dad, it was good enough for me. Let's see, what exactly did I have so far?

Alan Dennis was Jason Allan's father. He left Jason's mother before Jason was born.

Jason never knew who his father was because his mother wouldn't talk about it.

Alan arranged for Jason to move to Tregar Court, and paid his rent.

According to Jackie Langford, Alan Dennis and Jason's mother had split up because of financial troubles. This coincided with what Jason's sister, Sarah, had said.

Alan Dennis had gone to great lengths to try to make amends for walking out on his son. A son that by all accounts he may not even have known he had until later in life. He'd paid Jason's rent, and most likely had given him other money too. How else could Jason have afforded to live in Tregar Court? Alan had done all of this without ever letting Jason know who he was, and Jason had never suspected.

I had all of this, but still no real answers. There were still several pieces of the jigsaw missing:
- Why had Alan walked out on Jason's mum? What exactly had those money problems been?
- If Jason Allan had killed his father, why had he done it?
- Why didn't the CCTV show the murder?

It was time to take another look at the CCTV.
The same secretary who I'd met on my previous visit to

Gravesend Security collected me from reception.

"Here to see Tony again?"

"Yeah."

"I should warn you. He's not in a very good mood. He's been kind of depressed since his girlfriend dumped him. I think she must have sobered up and realised her mistake."

"Okay, thanks for the tip off."

She wasn't exaggerating. Tony looked as though he'd aged ten years since my last visit. His long hair was greasy and tied back into a ponytail. He hadn't shaved for at least a week, and he had a bad case of body odour.

"Why are you here again?" he growled.

"I just want another look at the tape."

"Waste of time."

"Still, if you don't mind."

He sighed as though life itself was too much bother.

This time around, I watched every frame over and over again. Tony had shown me how to control the film, so I was able to play it back and forth and to slow it down. After thirty minutes, I still hadn't seen anything new. Tony had barely spoken two words since I'd started to view the CCTV footage. He kept staring at his phone. At one point, I thought he was about to burst into tears. He put his phone down on the desk, grabbed a tissue and blew his nose. That's when I spotted the screen's wallpaper—it was a photograph of a woman—a woman I recognised.

He must have noticed me looking at the photo, so he grabbed the phone. "I have to go to the loo," he said, and slunk away.

I focussed on the CCTV again. There had to be something

I'd missed.

Eureka! I paused the film and zoomed in as close as I could. Mr Dixon, who had been standing with his wife at the back of the lift, scratched his chin. As he did so, the expensive watch on his right wrist was visible. I hated those men's watches which were so cluttered with dials that it was almost impossible to tell the time. Fortunately for me, this one also showed the day—*Wednesday*.

I had to be quick. Tony would be back at any moment. I navigated my way back to the main menu which listed the tapes by day/date. The murder had taken place on a Thursday, so why had Dixon's watch shown it to be Wednesday? His watch could have been wrong—it happened all the time. Or—

"What are you doing?" Tony grabbed my hand.

I turned to face him, and cast the 'forget' spell, followed by the 'sleep' spell. He slumped onto his seat, and I continued to work my way through the tapes for that same week. Monday—nothing unusual, Tuesday—nothing unusual, Wednesday—I hit pay dirt.

I watched as the Dixons got into the lift on the fourth floor. The victim got in on the third floor. This time the lift doors *did* open on the second floor, and Alan Dennis took a step back. He'd been trying to avoid the knife which had been thrust towards him from someone standing just outside the lift. The lift doors closed. On the next floor, Darcy James boarded the lift. On the ground floor, Alan Dennis fell headfirst through the open doors.

The tapes had obviously been switched, and I thought I knew why. I had to let Maxwell know, but first I had to pay another visit to Tregar Court.

The friendly concierge nodded to me as I walked into reception.

"Is Darcy James in?"

"I think so."

"Is it okay if I go up?"

"Sure, but the lift is being serviced at the moment. You'll have to take the stairs."

Great. Like my feet weren't aching enough after all the punishment they'd taken at the garden party.

I bumped into the cleaner on the first floor.

"Oh, hello." She was dusting the skirting boards with very little enthusiasm. "Back again?"

"Yes. Just tying up a few loose ends."

"I can't believe that young man did it," she said. "He seemed so timid."

"How has his girlfriend taken it?"

"Girlfriend?"

"Darcy James, the woman on the this floor."

"I didn't realise she was his girlfriend."

Now I was totally confused. "I thought you said you'd seen him sneaking into her room?"

"No, not him. I meant that old letch on the fourth floor."

"Mr Dixon?"

"Yeah. Right old pervert. Tried to grab me once, but I told him if he didn't pack it in, I'd set my Alfie on him."

"Let me get this straight. You've seen Mr Dixon going into Darcy James's apartment?"

"Oh, yeah. Several times. I don't think his wife knows. She'd probably kill him."

Now my head was spinning again. It was back to the A4 pad for me.

I only just remembered to pick up a can of pink salmon on my way back to the office. Just as well because Winky was on me as soon as I walked through the door.

"I've been thinking," he said, as he made short work of the salmon. "I think you should let those geezers next door move into this office."

"Geezers? Since when did you use words like geezer?"

"I'm a talking cat, and you're quibbling about my vocabulary?"

"Point taken. But no. Why should I let them take my office?"

"Look." He waved his paw around. "This place is a dump."

"It is not a dump. It has character."

"It's falling to pieces. Look, that guy Armitage seems pretty desperate. I'm sure he'll make it worth your while to move."

"I'm not interested."

"And I know just the place. It's much more modern, and spacious, and is very cat friendly."

I began to smell a cat. "By any chance, would the offices you have in mind be anywhere near Bella?"

"Funny you should say that—"

Chapter 21

Three hours later, and the Tregar case was still giving me a headache. I studied my scribblings on my trusty A4 pad. What exactly did I know *now*?

I'd solved the mystery of the CCTV. The digital recordings had been switched — the one seen by the police had actually been from the day before the murder took place. The wallpaper photo I'd seen on Tony's phone at Gravesend Security had been of Darcy James. On my first visit there, the secretary I'd spoken to had mentioned her surprise that Tony was dating such an attractive woman. Darcy James must have deliberately hooked up with him before the murder, so that she could persuade him to make the switch when the time came. She'd dumped him now, but he could hardly go to the police without implicating himself. The two recordings, the one from the day before the murder and the one on the day of the murder, were almost identical. The victim, the Dixons and Darcy James had been wearing the same clothes on both days, and they had stood in exactly the same position — almost as though it had been choreographed. The CCTV of the actual murder did not reveal the murderer's identity, but I was beginning to think that Jason Allan may well have been the person who delivered the deadly blow. The question was 'why'? I now knew he hadn't acted alone. Darcy James was implicated because of her actions with regard to the CCTV. According to the concierge, she'd had a relationship with Jason Allan, and according to the cleaner, she'd also had a relationship with Mr Dixon. Quite the busy girl our Darcy! But what about the Dixons? What was their involvement?

I should have taken the new information to Maxwell—particularly the info on the CCTV. If Sushi hadn't been on the scene, I probably would have, but I didn't want to give her the chance to shoot me down in flames. I needed more. I had to find the motive for the murder, and exactly who, apart from Jason Allan, had been involved.

It was getting late, and my eyelids were heavy. Time to call it a night.

The Tregar case was still buzzing around my head the next morning. I'd even had a nightmare in which I'd been trapped in a lift with the Dixons and Darcy James. My father once told me that sometimes you had to take a step back and allow your brain time to work things out for itself. At the time he'd said it, I hadn't given it much credence, but as I'd got more into the job, I'd seen the wisdom of his words. The facts of the case were already implanted in my brain. Staring at the A4 pad wasn't going to produce an answer. I needed to get away for a while. That would allow my brain to do its magic in the background. Where better to get away from it all than in Candlefield, and what better way to relax than to take Barry for a walk?

Who was I kidding?

"Barry! Leave those ducks alone! Barry! Leave that cat alone. Barry! Come back here! Barry! Put that down—you can't eat that!"

The dog was a nightmare, and I was exhausted. And now, he'd disappeared altogether. If he was in the swamp again, I was going to kill him. I hurried down the hill.

"Hello!" A female voice called to me.

I pulled up sharply, and turned to see a young witch,

about the same age as me, standing with two almost identical dogs. One of them was Barry.

"Is this your dog?" she shouted.

I nodded while trying to catch my breath.

"He seems to have taken a shine to Bonny."

"I thought he'd gone into the swamp again." I'd just about caught my breath.

"I'm Tess." She held out her hand.

"Jill." Her hand felt cold in mine.

"These two seem to have hit it off. What's his name?"

"Barry."

"Barry and Bonny? Oh, dear." She studied my face. "Don't I know you from somewhere?"

"I live above Cuppy C. It's a cake shop and tea room. Do you know it?"

"Yes, but I've never been in. Wait, wasn't your picture in The Candle? That's it, I remember now. You found the Candlefield Cup."

I nodded. "Do you live around here?"

"I have a small flat near to the main square. It's just about big enough for me and Bonny. I spend most of my time in the human world though—in a place called Washbridge. Do you know it?"

"I should. I've lived there all of my life."

"Really? Wow, that is a coincidence. What do you do there?"

"I'm a private investigator."

"Of course, it said as much in The Candle article. How exciting."

"Not really. What about you?"

"Oh, nothing nearly as glamorous. I'm a lawyer in Washbridge."

"That must be interesting."

"Most of it is routine. Maybe we could meet up in Washbridge some time? Get coffee or lunch?"

"Sure. Why not?" We exchanged phone numbers.

"I suppose I'd better be going then." Tess gave Bonny's lead a slight tug. "Catch you later."

I had to hold on tight to Barry's lead to stop him charging after his new girlfriend.

"Let me go," he pined. "I like her. Let me go."

"Bonny has to go home now." I turned and started walking back up the hill.

"I want to see her again." Barry planted his feet, so I had to drag him along.

"You will." I glanced back over my shoulder, expecting to see Tess and Bonny making their way to the exit, but they were nowhere to be seen. How was that possible? Where had they gone? There were no trees or bushes to obscure the view, and they hadn't had time to reach the exit. Perhaps she'd used a spell to speed her and Bonny along? Oh well, not to worry. It looked as though Barry might have found himself a girlfriend, and I'd found another witch who lived and worked in Washbridge. It might be nice to meet up with someone with whom I could talk openly—a little witch chit chat.

The walk back to the gates of the park was hard work. Barry was complaining and digging his heels in most of the way.

"Come on, Barry."

"When will I see Bonny again?"

"Soon."

"Do you promise?"

"Only if you walk properly now."

"Okay then, but you promised."

What was it with my pets and their love lives? Wasn't it bad enough that Winky was trying to get me to move offices so he could be closer to his beloved Bella? Now I had to put up with Barry fawning all over his new love. It was probably just as well that I didn't have a love life to speak of. When would I have had time for it?

We'd no sooner walked out of the park than I spotted a familiar figure in the distance.

"Lester!" I shouted.

He glanced around, and I felt sure that he'd seen me, but he hurried away in the opposite direction—ducking out of sight down a side street. The twins had mentioned that Aunt Lucy had been out of sorts, and even Grandma had noticed, but when I'd tried to talk to Aunt Lucy about it, she'd just changed the subject. If Lester had decided to end the relationship, the very least he could do was to come clean and tell her.

"Come on, Barry." I set off in pursuit.

"What about my food?"

"Later. Come on, we have to hurry."

Thankfully, Barry decided to play ball, and we ran down the street, but when we turned onto the side road, there was no sign of Lester.

"Find him boy," I said.

"Find who?" Barry gave me a blank stare.

"Lester."

"Where is he?"

"I want you to find him."

"How am I supposed to do that?"

"I don't know. You're a dog. Isn't that what dogs do?"

He shrugged.

"Never mind. Let's go home."

"For food?"

"Yes, for food."

There was no doubt in my mind that Lester had seen me, and had deliberately legged it. But why? He'd seemed so keen on Aunt Lucy at first, and had struck me as a nice, genuine guy. What had changed? As far as I was aware, there hadn't been a bust-up of any kind. I had the impression that Aunt Lucy was as bewildered as everyone else by his behaviour. What was I supposed to do now? Should I tell Aunt Lucy that I'd seen him, and that he'd run away? That wasn't going to make her feel any better, and would probably only make matters worse. I decided to keep it to myself until I could corner Lester and get some straight answers from him.

After I'd fed Barry, I bumped into the twins who had obviously been waiting for me.

"Jill, you have to help us," Amber said.

This was becoming a familiar theme. How had they coped before I came on the scene, I wondered?

"What's wrong now?"

"It's Miles," Pearl said.

I laughed.

"It's not funny!"

"Yeah, it's not funny, Jill," Amber said.

"Oh, come on. It's a little bit funny. The two of you both had a secret crush on sexy, handsome Miles, only to find out that he'd turned into a bald blob. That's a little bit funny isn't it?"

They both glared at me.

"I guess not. What exactly is it you want me to do?"

"Get rid of him. He comes around here every day, and he

won't take a hint."

"Why don't you tell him straight that you're not interested?"

"We've tried. He won't listen. He says he knows we were both sweet on him back at school."

"You were, weren't you?"

"Apparently." Amber glared at her sister.

"Don't blame me. I didn't know he was interested in you too."

"How am I supposed to get rid of him?" I said. "What makes you think he'll listen to me if he won't listen to you?"

"Well —" Amber hesitated.

"We thought —" Pearl began.

"Come on. Spit it out."

"Well," Amber said. "You know how to do the 'transform' spell."

I didn't like the direction this was going in — not one bit.

"No! Don't even think about it."

I'd cast the level five, 'transform' spell once at the Spell-Range, but Grandma had said I'd made a mess of it by turning a donkey into a toad instead of a frog.

"You have to," Pearl said. "It's the only way to get rid of him."

"I don't *believe* you two. Do you really think I'm going to turn some poor guy into a frog just because he's bald and fat?"

The twins looked at one another, and then back at me.

"Yes."

"Definitely."

Unbelievable.

"I'll have a word with him, but I'm not going to turn him

into a frog—"

"What about a rat?" Amber said.

"I'm not going to turn him into anything! Got it?"

They both pouted.

"Do you want me to have a word with him or not?"

They nodded.

"Then stop acting like children."

"Sorry."

"Sorry."

I wondered if I should mention having seen Lester to the twins, but I didn't trust them to keep it to themselves. If they let it slip to Aunt Lucy it would only upset her more, and if they let it slip to Grandma—well that didn't even bear thinking about.

As if my to-do list wasn't long enough already, now I had to talk down love-struck Miles too.

Chapter 22

I'd gone to Candlefield to relax, and in the hope that my subconscious might come up with some brilliant revelation on the Tregar case. Epic fail! Not only was I no nearer to solving that case, but I now had to worry about what was happening with Lester, and how to get Miles off the twins' backs. Still, it was nice to know that some things never changed. Mrs V was still knitting. A blue sock today, if I wasn't mistaken. And Winky was still waving his little flags around.

Magic was great, but sometimes what was needed was good old fashioned research. I fired up the computer and turned to my trusty friend in times of need: Google. I spent the best part of two hours using every combination of search terms I could come up with until I finally caught a break, and that was more by luck than judgement. I'd been searching for anything I could find on 'Alan Dennis', and combining that with terms such as: 'bankrupt' and 'financial scam'. After ploughing through page after page of results which turned out to be dead ends, I spotted a result for a Dennis Allan rather than Alan Dennis. I wasn't optimistic, but clicked on the link anyway. It took me to an archived edition of a local newspaper. The story was about a Ponzi scheme which had led to the financial ruin of numerous 'investors'. Apparently the 'mastermind' behind the scam had fled the country before the police could apprehend him. There were a few quotes from some of those who'd been affected. One of those came from a Mr Dennis Allan who was quoted as saying that he'd lost everything.

It was a long shot, but it was all I had to go on. I did a

search on 'Dennis Allan'. This time I was only interested in the images which the search threw up. Who knew there were so many men with that name? Once again I ploughed through page after page of photos. I almost missed the black and white group photograph, but a face in the third row caught my eye. I clicked on the image to see the original web page. The photograph had been taken almost thirty five years ago. Three rows of young men, all dressed in black graduation robes, were smiling at the camera. Their names were listed underneath the image. Sure enough, there on the third row, fifth from the left was the face of Alan Dennis—the victim in the lift. Or as he had been known back then, Dennis Allan.

Slowly it all began to slip into place. Dennis Allan had been an educated man who by all accounts had been in a well-paid job. Despite this, he'd fallen victim to a Ponzi scheme. He'd lost everything and, presumably because of the stress or shame, had walked out on his partner, unaware that she was pregnant with his child. He'd changed his name from Dennis Allan to Alan Dennis, and had started afresh. He'd worked his way back up the ladder and had become quite wealthy by working as an accountant for a number of rich clients. Somewhere along the way, he must have found out about his son, and had taken it upon himself to make amends by helping him financially. For reasons known only to himself, Alan Dennis never let Jason Allan know that he was his father.

At long last, it felt like I might be getting somewhere. I spent the next hour researching Ponzi schemes. It didn't make pretty reading. Essentially the pattern was always the same: promises too good to be true, gullible people—not necessarily uneducated—it seemed that even the most intelligent person could be gullible if enough money was at stake. This was inevitably followed by financial ruin. The perpetrators of the fraud were rarely caught. Usually they had fled the country with their ill-gotten gains before the house of cards came tumbling down. There were just a few cases where those responsible had been brought to justice. One story in particular, from twenty years ago, caught my eye. A man and wife had been arrested for fraud — the article included a photograph of the pair being led into court. I recognised their faces. Now everything was beginning to make sense.

The door to my office opened, and in walked Kathy.
"Hope you don't mind me gatecrashing," she said.
"As if I could stop you. What brings you into town?"
"Have you forgotten already? I started my new job this morning."
I'd tried to blank out the idea of Kathy working in Grandma's wool shop. "How bad was it?"
"It was fun. You can't imagine how nice it is to do something other than housework."
"What about Grandma though?"
"She's a darling."
I laughed. "No, seriously. Just how horrible was she?"
"She's been really sweet to me. She said she knew I'd been out of the job market for a long time, and that I should take my time to settle in."
"Are you sure we're talking about the same woman? Warty nose? Crooked fingers?"
"That's just cruel. I think you're being unfair to your grandmother. To hear you talk, anyone would think she was some kind of witch."

"So what is it you want?"

"Charming." Kathy did her best to look affronted. "What makes you think I want something? Can't I just be paying a social call during my lunch break?"

"Very unlikely."

"Well, actually there is something."

"I knew it. It had better not be a circus."

"It isn't."

"Or theatre."

"As if."

"Or a garden party."

"That reminds me, I meant to ask you. How on earth did you manage to win those toys for the kids?"

"Never mind that. What kind of nightmare have you signed me up for this time?"

"I haven't signed you up for anything. It's our anniversary soon. Peter and me thought it would be nice if we could go away for the weekend."

"That'll be nice. The kids will enjoy a break."

"That's just it. We were hoping it could be just the two of us. We thought you could look after the kids."

"Me? All weekend?"

"It would only be one night. We'd leave on a Saturday morning and be back Sunday evening."

"What am I meant to do with them?"

"You'll think of something."

"The kids won't want to stay with me."

"They do. We've already checked with them. We told them Auntie Jill will find lots of exciting things for them to do. So, what do you say?"

"Do I have a choice?"

"Of course not."

"That's what I figured."

Kathy ate her lunch while telling me all about her morning at Ever A Wool Moment.

"Have you seen the Everlasting Wool?" She asked through a mouthful of bread and cheese.

"Yeah. I won a subscription for Mrs V."

"How does it work?"

I shrugged.

"I can't figure it out," Kathy said. "It's like some kind of magic."

If only I could prove it.

Kathy practically skipped out of the office. The cynic in me wondered how long that would last. Grandma would show her true colours sooner or later. Then we'd see if Kathy still thought she was 'sweet'.

It was the Levels Competition on Saturday, but first I still had a case to crack. I put in a call to the concierge at Tregar. If I wasn't mistaken, he seemed to have taken quite a shine to me. I needed him to be my eyes and ears, and to report back to me.

Bingo! He readily agreed to my request and promised to give me a call at the appropriate time.

I'd no sooner ended my call to him, than the phone rang.

"Is that Jill?" a female voice said.

"Speaking."

"It's Tess. We met in the park. With the dogs."

"Oh, yeah. I remember. Hi."

"I know you're probably busy, but I wondered if you'd like to grab lunch or a coffee on Friday?"

"Coffee would probably be better. What time?"

"After work would be best for me. How about six?"

"That works for me."

We arranged to meet at a small coffee shop that I'd walked past numerous times before, but never been in. According to Tess, they made the best lattes in Washbridge.

Until I got a call from the concierge, there wasn't much more I could do on the Tregar case. I'd hardly had time to think about the Levels Competition, and time was running out. I didn't want to be on the wrong end of Grandma's anger by messing up. From what I'd been told, witches could be asked to demonstrate any spell from the level corresponding to the round of the competition. So, in round one, the spell would be a level one spell. In round two it would be a level two spell, and so on. I wasn't too worried about the level one spells. Looking back now, they all seemed incredibly simple. The level two spells were more difficult, but I was confident with at least seventy five per cent of them. According to Aunt Lucy, it was taken as read that any witch put forward into the competition would have the ability to cast the spells. What was more important was the 'quality' of the spell. As Grandma was always emphasising, and as I'd now come to realise, the same spell could be cast by three different witches, but with very different results. It was all about the focus.

Time to practise. I fed Winky, and told Mrs V that I'd be out for the rest of the day. There were several spells which weren't really suited to practise at home or anywhere in Washbridge for that matter. It was time to get serious — time to pay another visit to the Spell-Range.

I'd only been there once before, and that had been with Grandma and the twins. I considered asking the twins to join me, but thought better of it. As much as I liked the girls, they didn't really take their witchcraft seriously. They were more interested in Cuppy C, and their fiancés. As far as I could tell, neither of them had any burning ambition to progress beyond level two.

The Spell-Range was much quieter than on my previous visit. There were only three other witches and two wizards in the whole place. That suited me. I was still a little self-conscious when practising spells—particularly those which were new to me or which I'd only used occasionally. I found a quiet corner and took out the book of spells which I'd brought with me. I'd put a yellow Post-it note on the pages of the five spells I felt least confident in.

Three hours, and a lot of mental anguish later, I felt as though I'd mastered all of them except one. I couldn't seem to get to grips with the 'magnet' spell. The basic idea was that it should turn my hand into a magnet which would attract a metal object. Simple huh? Well, you might think so, but you'd be wrong. The devil was in the detail. The whole idea of the spell was that I should be able to attract a *specific* metal object not *all* metal objects. There was no shortage of resources at the Spell-Range, so it was easy to assemble a collection of metal objects: a horse shoe, a kettle, a knife, an empty can, and a dozen other bits and pieces. I was supposed to be able to attract just one of those objects without moving the others, but every time I cast the spell, all of the objects came hurtling towards me. I had to reverse the spell quickly to avoid being stabbed by the knife. I was on my fifth attempt, and still hadn't mastered it.

"Aren't you Jill Gooder?" a squeaky voice behind me said.

I turned around, expecting to see a woman, but the voice belonged to a skinny, young wizard.

"That's right."

"I thought I recognised you."

"And you are?"

"None of your business."

Another graduate of charm school. "Did you want something?"

"Are you competing in the Levels?" He wiped a finger across his snotty nose.

"Yes, why?"

"It shouldn't be allowed. You haven't been a witch for five minutes."

"Technically speaking that's incorrect. I was a —"

"Don't come your clever ways with me. Newcomers aren't wanted in the Levels."

"I'm sorry you feel that way. Now, if you'll excuse me."

"Don't matter anyway. If that's the best you can do with the 'magnet' spell, you ain't got no chance."

I let the double negative go. "Okay. Thanks for the feedback."

"You're up against Alicia Dawes. She's a *real* witch. You don't stand a chance — might as well pack up and go home now." With that, he walked away.

Cheeky sod. Who did he think he was? I cast the 'magnet' spell, giving it every ounce of concentration I had. The horseshoe flew across the ground and landed on my hand. The other objects stayed put. Yes! Put that in your pipe and smoke it, Alicia Dawes — whoever you are.

Chapter 23

I arrived at Christy's bakery at a little after four in the
morning. If my timing was right, I'd be there just after
Gary, the dispatch man, had clocked off, but before the
delivery drivers arrived. The only people around were the
cleaning crew, and they had moved into the offices.

The delivery vans were parked in the dispatch area, which
was just inside the building. I hid underneath the metal
staircase, which led up to the offices, and waited. A few
moments later, I heard footsteps. It was only three
minutes after four — too early for the delivery drivers. A
key turned in a lock, and then one of the van's back doors
opened. Moments later it closed again. Someone had
climbed inside one of the vans.

It wasn't difficult to pick out the right van because I could
see a slight movement, as whoever was inside shifted
around. As quietly as I could, I made my way across the
dispatch area until I was directly behind the van in
question. I took hold of the handle, and opened the door.

Just as I'd suspected!

Beryl Christy passed me a cup of tea. We were in her
office overlooking the factory floor.

"How did you know it was me?" she said.

"You still have Eddie Lingard on your payroll. That didn't
make any sense, so I tried to figure out why you would
still be paying him. I could only come up with two
possible explanations. Either he was blackmailing you, or
you felt guilty for dismissing him. After meeting him, I
came to the conclusion he wasn't the blackmailing type.
Even so, I wasn't absolutely sure my hunch was right

until I opened the van door just now."

"Eddie was one of the best employees I've ever had. He worked his socks off. He came in early and stayed late."

"Which is why you had to dismiss him."

"Yes. I wouldn't have had time to get to the cakes before the drivers arrived if Eddie had still been working here."

"And you kept on paying him?"

"What else could I do? None of this was his fault. I couldn't let Annie sell the business. This bakery is my life. What would I do without it?"

"Why didn't you just tell her that you didn't want to sell?"

"I *have* tried, believe me, but she's got it into her head that running the business is too much for me."

"Is it?"

"No. I love it. It's what gets me out of bed in the morning."

"Then why sabotage it and risk losing your customers?"

"I thought if I could do just enough damage to put off the buyer, that I'd be able to win those customers back later. Stupid, I know, but I wasn't thinking straight." She hesitated. "I suppose you'll have to tell Annie and the twins?"

"Not necessarily, but only if you agree to certain conditions."

"Go on."

"You have to stop the sabotage — right now."

"Of course. You can't imagine how painful it's been for me to damage my beautiful cakes."

"And you have to tell Annie that you don't want to sell the business. Tell her what you've just told me — that the business is your life, and you can't bear the thought of giving it up."

"But what if she won't listen?"

"You have to make her listen, or I'll spill the beans. Okay?"

"Okay. I'll do it."

As I was already up at such a ridiculous hour, I decided to kill two birds with one stone. Bakers weren't the only ones who kept crazy hours. The first edition of The Candle newspaper should have been coming off the press about now. I'd had some dealings with reporters in Washbridge, and knew that many of them kept ludicrously unsocial hours. On the off chance that I'd catch one of them at their desk, I slipped through the deserted reception area and soon located the news floor.

It seemed I was wrong—every desk was deserted. Oh well. I'd have to try again later.

"Hello?" A vampire wearing a baggy, sleeveless jumper over a shirt—not a good look—appeared out of a small office to my right. "Who are you?"

"Jill Gooder." I walked over to him. As I got closer, I saw he was wearing Bermuda shorts. Nice combo.

"What do you want?" He took a long drag on a cigar—totally ignoring the 'No Smoking' signs posted all around the office.

"I'm a private investigator."

"So? Do you want a medal?"

"I just wanted to ask a few questions. You are?"

"Terry Hosser. I'm the editor-in-chief, if it's any of your business."

Mr T Hosser was certainly living up to his name. "It won't take long. If I could just have a few moments of your time."

"I'm leaving in five minutes. What do you want to know?"

"I've been looking through the archives of your publication, and I can find no mention of TDO at all. Can you explain that?"

"What's to explain? We report the news."

"But surely TDO is news? He's cast a shadow over Candlefield for years now. He's been responsible for several deaths, and yet no one even knows who or what he is."

"And what's your interest in this exactly?"

"I'm a resident of Candlefield. I think it would be in the public interest for you to report on this issue. Surely it is exactly the kind of thing that begs the attention of investigative journalism."

"If you *were* a resident of Candlefield, I might hear you out, but isn't it true that you spend most of your time in the human world? What gives you the right to tell full-time sups how we should live or what we should do? I know who you are. You're sticking your nose into places it doesn't belong. Look, I'm going to do you a favour and give you some free advice. Leave TDO alone. It will be better for you, and for the people of Candlefield."

"That sounds like a threat."

"It's just friendly advice. Now, if you don't mind I have a home to go to."

That seemed to confirm my suspicions. For whatever reason, news about TDO was being deliberately suppressed. Whether that was through fear and intimidation or collusion, I didn't know. But I intended to make it my business to find out.

I arrived at Cuppy C just as Christy's van had been unloaded.

"Jill?" Amber said through a yawn. "What are you doing up at this hour?"

The twins took it in turns to get up early to meet the deliveries.

"I wanted to let you know that you shouldn't have any more problems with the deliveries from Christy's."

"Really? What happened? Who was doing it?"

"I can't give you any details, I'm afraid."

"Why not?"

"Because if I did, I'd have to kill you."

Amber managed a tired smile. "Oh, well. As long as it's sorted, I guess that's all that matters. Do you want to come in for a drink? We aren't actually open yet, but you get special treatment."

I wasn't about to say no. My body still hadn't forgiven me for dragging it out of bed so early. An injection of coffee and a toasted teacake might revive me.

After Amber had unloaded the delivery, she joined me at the back table. We were both munching on delicious, hot, buttery teacakes.

"You toast a mean teacake," I said.

"Thanks. It *is* pretty good although I do say so myself."

"Is Pearl still in bed?"

"What do you think? It should have been her turn this morning, but last night she said she was feeling a little queasy. She's such a liar."

"I was not lying." Pearl appeared, still dressed in her polka dot nightie. "I did feel queasy."

"Are you okay now?" I asked.

"Yes, thanks."

"Of course she's okay. All the work's been done now by yours truly."

"I'll cover for you tomorrow and the day after."

"You bet your life you will."

Oh boy. It was too early for this. "I just told Amber that the Christy problem is solved."

"Really?" Pearl yawned. "How?"

"She can't tell you," Amber said. "Or she'd have to kill you."

Pearl joined us at the table and reached over to take a piece of teacake from her sister's plate.

"Hey!" Amber slapped her hand away. "Make your own."

"Have a piece of mine," I offered.

"It's okay, Jill," Pearl said. "If meanie-pants here won't share, I'll make my own later."

Amber poked out her tongue at her sister.

"How's the Miles situation?" I asked.

When would I learn to keep my big mouth shut?

"He came around again yesterday," Pearl said.

"You have to do something soon. He's driving us crazy."

They gave me his address minus the house number.

"What number does he live at?"

"I can't remember, sorry. It's a small cul-de-sac—you won't have any problems finding him. Just ask where the fat, bald guy lives."

Harsh but true.

I promised I'd do what I could.

"He's been nosing around again," Mrs V said.

"Who?"

"That Armitage guy from next door. He said he thought he'd dropped something in your office when he visited with the landlord."

"Dropped what?"

"A pen."

"Did he see Winky?"

"No. I wouldn't let him go through. I said I'd take a look around and let him have his pen if I found it. He wasn't very pleased, but he wasn't going to get past me."

"Good for you, Mrs V. Did you find it?"

"I didn't bother looking. I could tell he was lying because his eyebrows twitched. Next time he comes here, he'll feel the sharp end of my knitting needles."

I laughed. Who needed a guard dog when they had a Mrs V?

CoffeeDrops had to be one of the smallest coffee shops in Washbridge. Although I'd walked past it numerous times, I'd never actually ventured inside. Tess was waiting for me by the door when I arrived.

"Sorry I'm late," I said, still trying to catch my breath.

"No problem. I've only just got here myself."

I'd have been on time if Winky hadn't waylaid me with a report he'd compiled of all the reasons we should relocate to new offices. I'd dumped that in the trash on my way over to the coffee shop.

Tess looked every inch the young professional. When I'd seen her in the park in Candlefield, she'd been dressed in jeans, jumper and boots. Today, she was wearing a smart, black suit.

She insisted on ordering and paying for the drinks. On her recommendation, I had the caramel latte.

"What kind of lawyer are you?" I asked.

"Mergers and Acquisitions mainly. Pretty boring stuff."

"Sounds complicated."

"Not really. Just lots of long days and late nights. Still, the pay is good so I shouldn't complain."

"What made you decide to work in the—" I lowered my voice to a whisper. "In the human world?"

"I guess I wanted to see both worlds. Most of my friends have never been outside Candlefield. I can't imagine spending my whole life among only sups. I kind of like humans. I've even dated a couple."

"Are you with someone now?"

"Not at the moment. What about you?"

"Not that you'd notice."

We talked for almost an hour. Just like me, Tess maintained two homes. She had what sounded like a top-end apartment in the centre of Washbridge—close to her offices. In Candlefield, she had a small flat near to the main square. She described herself as cash rich, time poor. That's why she employed a cleaner in both Washbridge and Candlefield. She also paid someone to look after, and walk Bonny. She was a smart cookie and clearly had her life together. Just like me. What? What's so funny about that?

"Where's the loo in here?" I said.

"It's up the spiral staircase." Tess checked her watch. "Look if you don't mind, I need to get off. There's a deal we have to close tonight."

"Sure."

"Maybe we can do this again some time?"

"Definitely."

When I got back to my seat, Tess had gone. I drank what was left of my latte and then headed home. Tomorrow was the Levels Competition. A few hours spent on last minute revision was called for.

Chapter 24

I felt like death, or something bearing an uncanny resemblance to it. My legs and arms ached—so did my head. And I felt like I hadn't slept for a month, which was weird because I'd only just climbed out of bed. I'd started to feel a little weary the previous night while I'd been doing last minute revision for the competition, but I'd put that down to having had an early start at the bakery. It felt like I had flu, but I didn't have any kind of head cold. Of all the days for this to happen, it had to be today. What was I supposed to do? I wasn't sure I could drag myself across the living room let alone all the way to Candlefield to take part in a competition. What was the alternative? To call Grandma and tell her I couldn't make it? She wouldn't believe I was ill, and even if she did, would she care? Not a chance. Somehow, some way, I had to get to the competition and hope that I'd feel better as the day went on.

It was two hours later, and I'd made it to Candlefield. How? I had no idea. If anything I was feeling slightly worse.

Grandma was waiting for me outside the Spell-Range as agreed. The whole area was already bustling with people. Bunting, flags and banners had been hung from the walls and the lampposts.

"I didn't think you were coming," she said.

"Sorry I'm late." Even my jaw ached. "I'm not feeling too well."

"Were you drinking last night?"

"No! I was revising."

"What's the matter with you then?" She stepped closer and put her crooked fingers on my forehead. "You're burning up. Open your mouth."

I did.

"Say Arrrh."

"Arrrh."

"Just as I thought!" she said.

"What?"

"You've been poisoned."

"What? How?"

"Never mind that now. We need to get it out of your system."

I didn't like the sound of that. I didn't like the sound of that one little bit.

"Come with me." She grabbed me by the hand, cast a spell, and the next thing I knew we were in her kitchen. "Sit down!"

I didn't need telling twice. My legs were all set to give way anyway.

Grandma took several jars from her cupboard and poured the contents into a large pan which she heated on a low light. Next she grabbed a bag from under the sink and picked out something which looked remarkably like a cockroach, and threw it into the pan. After a few minutes, she poured the liquid from the pan into a large mug.

"Drink this."

The smell almost made me retch.

"I can't."

"Drink it or I'll pour it down your throat."

She wasn't joking. I picked up the mug, and closed my eyes. If I'd been able to see the horrible concoction, there'd have been no way I could have drunk it. I took a sip.

"Yuk!" I spat it out. "I can't drink—"

Before I could finish the sentence, she'd grabbed my nose, pushed my head back, and poured the liquid down my throat.

I danced around the kitchen with my mouth wide open— trying desperately to get rid of the taste and smell.

"Any minute now," Grandma said. "You're going to be— "

I put my head over the sink and threw up. For the next twenty minutes, I continued to throw up until I was certain there was nothing left inside me.

"Sit down." She took my hand, led me into the living room, and lowered me onto the sofa. "How do you feel?"

"Like I just died."

"You might well have done if you hadn't got that out of your system. You can have ten minutes, and then we have to get back or you'll lose your place in the competition."

"Are you kidding? I can't possibly compete now."

"Of course you can. You'll be fine now it's out of your system. You'll start to feel better soon."

I still felt terrible, but I could tell things were starting to improve. The aches in my arms and legs weren't as bad, and my headache was starting to ease. But I still felt as weak as a kitten.

"What was it?" I managed to say through dry lips.

"I'm not sure, but my guess would be Brewflower."

"What's that?"

"It's a rare plant that's been banned in Candlefield for several centuries, but there's still some to be had on the black market. It can be fatal in high doses, but more commonly it's used to put someone out of action for twenty-four to forty-eight hours. Someone didn't want you in the competition today." She checked her watch. "Come on. It's time we got back."

The inside of the Spell-Range was barely recognisable. Bleachers had been installed on three sides. They were already almost full to capacity. I tried to pick out Aunt Lucy or the twins, but it was impossible. Stalls selling all manner of refreshments were lined up along the remaining wall, and were already doing a roaring trade. Row after row of small cubicles had been installed for the competitors. Grandma led me to the one that had my name on the front.

"How are you feeling?" she asked, as she ushered me inside.

"Much better. Just hungry."

"It's probably better you don't eat until the competition is over. Now, you'd better get changed."

"Why do I need to change?"

"You didn't think you could compete wearing those did you?"

I glanced at my jeans and tee-shirt. "What's wrong with these?"

"The Levels is the most prestigious competition held for witches. Competitors are expected to wear traditional clothes." She handed me a long black smock dress and a pointed hat.

"This is a joke, right?" I laughed.

"Do I look like I'm joking?"

She didn't.

"But this is the sort of thing that witches wear in children's books."

"Where do you think those authors got their ideas from?"

"You mean witches really used to wear these?"

"Going back centuries, yes. Nowadays standards have dropped, and they're only worn on occasions like this. Hurry up. We don't have all day."

I changed into the dress and hat. I looked as though I was on my way to a Halloween ball.

"Now you look like a witch," Grandma said, and almost smiled. "I've checked out the competition, and from what I can see you only really have one serious opponent. A third year, second-level witch name of Alicia Dawes."

"So I hear."

"You know her?"

"No, but I met someone yesterday who made it clear he didn't think I should be allowed to compete today. He mentioned her name."

"If you're on your game, you should be more than a match for her. But remember, what's the golden rule?"

"Focus."

"Very good. Now wait here until they call your name, and then you make your appearance. Understood?"

I nodded.

Grandma reached for the door.

"Aren't you going to wish me luck?"

"I don't believe in luck."

There wasn't a mirror in the cubicle so I couldn't get a good look at myself, but I was pretty sure I looked ridiculous. Maybe this was all some elaborate joke, and I'd just been punked.

"Ladies and Gentlemen." A man's voice bellowed over the loudspeakers. "We now come to the level two competition. This year we have five contestants. Please welcome, Hilary Love."

The crowd began to cheer.

"Next we have Sasha Newcombe."

Even louder cheering. I recognised Sasha's name from my visit to Eddie Lingard's house.

"Our third contestant is Marie King."

My hands were beginning to tremble.

"Our fourth contestant will be known to many of you already. Please welcome Jill Gooder."

I opened the door to a deafening cheer. I waved a hand to acknowledge the crowd, and then took a quick glance to my left at the other competitors. To my relief, they too were dressed in black smocks and pointed hats.

"And last, but not least, I give you your final level two contestant, Alicia Dawes."

I glanced to my right at the last cubicle. The handle turned, and the door opened. The final competitor stepped out to ear-shattering applause.

"Tess?" I gasped.

Tess or Alicia, or whatever her name really was, waved to the crowd. When the applause finally subsided, she turned to me. There was no emotion on her face.

"Tess?" I said again.

"I hope you're ready to lose," she spat the words. The friendly, smiling woman I'd had coffee with the day before was nowhere to be seen, and suddenly everything became clear.

"You poisoned me," I said.

She smiled, but said nothing.

The format of the competition was straightforward enough. Each of us had to perform the same spell, and at the end of each round the witch who'd performed worst was eliminated. There was a panel of three level six witches who would adjudicate.

In round one we were asked to perform the 'levitation' spell. We had to levitate to a particular height and then move back and forth, left and right following their precise instructions. Thanks to my improved focus, I now had much better control than the first time I'd attempted that particular spell when I'd ended up falling flat on my backside.

Sasha Newcombe was eliminated at the end of the first round. The judges gave no indication of how each competitor had done, so I wasn't sure how I'd faired against the others. In round two, we were asked to perform the 'lightning bolt' spell. A padded target in the shape of a giant owl (why an owl? I had no idea) was wheeled out in front of each of us. On the judges' command we had to cast the spell and then fire the lightning bolt at the poor old owl. This time it was pretty obvious who would be eliminated. The targets which Alicia and I had in front of us had almost entirely disintegrated. The target in front of Hilary Love was almost as devastated, but Marie King's target had only a small scorch mark on it. We were down to three. I didn't like the 'fireproof' spell. I'd only tried it a couple of times, and it had scared me both times. The spell should allow me to walk through fire unscathed, but having the courage to actually do it was another thing entirely. A line of fire was lit in front of us and we were given the go-ahead. I cast the spell, and focussed with all of my might. The three of us came through the other side unscathed — almost. Hilary Love had the slightest of singes on her fringe.

That left just me and Alicia in the competition.

"The final and deciding round," the head judge said, "will be the 'magnet' spell."

Great! One of my least favourite spells, and the one I felt least confident about.

"This is where you lose," Alicia said under her breath.

A large pile of metal objects was placed about ten yards in front of us.

"Contestants," the head judge said. "You are to attract the metal star which is on the top of the pile. Do you see it?"

We both nodded.

"Whichever one of you is able to attract the star will be the winner and will progress to the grand final. Are you ready?"

We nodded again.

"Go!"

The star rose from the pile, but then moved no further. Both of us had it under our control, so it would come down to whichever of us had the most focus. I closed my eyes and remembered everything that Grandma had taught me. Before today, I hadn't been too concerned how I did in the competition, but I'd be damned if I was going to let this cheating little cow beat me. I put everything I had into the spell.

The star hit my hand with such force it almost knocked me over. The crowd erupted.

"We have a winner." The head judge announced. "Jill Gooder is this year's level two champion."

I glanced to my right where Grandma was standing, and for a moment I thought I saw a smile cross her lips.

"You won!" Amber appeared from somewhere and threw her arms around me.

"I knew you would!" Pearl almost bowled me over.

"Well done!" Aunt Lucy said.

"Thanks everyone."

I glanced back at Alicia who looked as though she wanted to kill me.

"You're in the final," Amber said. "You could become a level six witch."

"Leave the girl alone." Grandma pushed the twins away. "She has to prepare. Go back to your seats."

"Good luck, Jill!"

"Good luck! We'll be rooting for you!"

The twins and Aunt Lucy made their way back to the bleachers.

"Aren't you pleased?" I said to Grandma. "I won!"

"Of course you did. I taught you, didn't I?"

Chapter 25

I sat with the winner of the level one competition while the rounds for levels three through to five played out. Although the witches at level three didn't seem that much more advanced, it was a totally different ball game at levels four and five. They brought 'focus' to a whole new level. The complexity, power and accuracy of the spells which they performed were mind-blowing.

"How are we meant to compete against that?" the level one winner said.

"We're not. They don't expect us to win the final. We're just there to make up the numbers."

"No witch under my supervision is there to make up the numbers!" Grandma said.

"Oh, hello, Grandma. I didn't see you there."

"Watch and learn." She pointed a crooked finger at the level five competitors who were down to the last two.

Thirty minutes later, and it was time for the grand final. The winners from each of the five levels stood side by side as we were once again introduced to the cheering crowd. Now I knew where the twins and Aunt Lucy were seated, I could see them cheering and waving their arms in the air.

The format was similar to the heats except that in each round the spell would be taken from the same level as the round number, so in round one the spell was a level one spell.

The head judge announced that the spell would be 'faster'. This would be a very simple spell to judge because we were all required to run to a given point on the other side of the Spell-Range and back. Each of us would be timed, and the slowest eliminated. It came as no major surprise that we finished in order of our levels. I finished next to last, and the level one witch was eliminated. In the second round, a level two spell was to be selected. The judges chose the 'Grow' spell. Maybe I did have a chance. I'd done rather well with that spell when I'd visited the Spell-Range with the twins, but there was far more pressure this time. We moved a few yards along the wall to a plot where four saplings had been planted. Again, this would be an easy spell to judge. The witch with the shortest plant after the spell had been cast would be eliminated. I glanced over at Grandma who mouthed the word: 'focus'.

The judge gave the command to start and I cast the spell. I kept my eyes closed until the command to stop was given. When I opened my eyes, I quickly studied the four trees. Those in front of the level four and five witches were much higher than mine, but there was barely anything between mine and that of the level three witch.

The judges all studied the trees, and then conferred among themselves.

"Level three witch, Norah Lane is eliminated."

Norah shook my hand, and said, "Well done. Good luck."

"Thanks."

I was now completely out of my comfort zone. Not only was I dealing with spells a level above mine, I was dealing with spells I'd never seen before. The head judge announced that I'd be allowed five minutes to study the 'propel' spell. In essence, the spell allowed us to propel an object through the air. The test was how accurately we were able to do that.

Grandma started to walk towards me, but was blocked by

one of the officials. I was on my own. The spell was many times more complex than the ones I was used to. I wasn't even sure I'd have it memorised in time, let alone be able to perform it with any accuracy. While I was studying the spell, three huge targets were wheeled into place approximately fifty yards away. At the same time, three huge metal spears were plunged into the soft ground in front of us.

"Time is up." The judge announced. "On my command, you must take control of the spear and fire it at your target."

I'd never performed a spell like this one, and I was terrified. Not of messing up the spell—I could live with that. I was worried that my spear might miss the target and hit someone in the crowd.

"Are you ready?"

I was tempted to deliberately make a mess of the spell, so that the spear would remain stuck in the ground, but the thought of what Grandma might do to me, meant that wasn't an option. Moments later, all three spears had extracted themselves, and were hovering parallel to the ground. At least I'd managed that part of the spell okay. Suddenly one of the spears flew across the ground and hit the bullseye. The level five witch smiled—justifiably satisfied with her work. The level four witch's spear was next to take flight. It too hit the target, but only on the very outer edge. All eyes were on me now.

"Come on, Jill!

"Go, Jill!"

"Jill, Jill, Jill!"

Although the crowd were trying to help, they only succeeded in making me even more nervous.

I had to focus. I had to shut out the noise of the crowd. I took note of where the target was, and then closed my eyes. Focus, I had to focus like I never had before. I opened my eyes as the spear began its flight. The crowd fell silent. Everything seemed to happen in slow motion as I waited.

The spear glanced the very edge of the target, but then fell to the ground. There was a huge gasp from the crowd, then a few moments of silence before the cheers erupted for the level four and five witches.

I'd been eliminated. The twins and Aunt Lucy came rushing over.

"You did brilliantly!" Amber screamed.

"You beat the level three witch!" Pearl shouted.

"Well done, Jill." Aunt Lucy beamed.

"I don't know why you are all so excited." Grandma pushed her way past the twins. "What do you call that? The level four witch left it wide open for you to take your place in the final."

"I did my best. I'd never even seen the spell before."

"That's no excuse. I expected much better from you." With that, she turned and walked away.

"Take no notice of her." My mother's ghost appeared at my side. "I know I said I'd only come when you called, but I couldn't miss your big day. You did really well. You should be proud of yourself."

"Thanks Mum. That means a lot."

We all stayed on to watch the rest of the competition. It came as no surprise that the level five witch was the eventual winner. It was well deserved, and she seemed delighted to be joining the ranks of the level six witches.

"That will be you one day," my mother said.

"I don't think so

"Mark my words. And it'll be sooner rather than later."

Back in the cubicle, I changed into my own clothes. I'd just finished getting ready when there was a knock on the door — probably Grandma to give me another dressing down.

I opened the door to find Alicia. Standing next to her was the skinny wizard who was obviously Alicia's fanboy.

"Hello, Alicia, or should I call you Tess?"

"You were lucky today," she said through gritted teeth.

"Lucky I didn't die from the poison you gave me, you mean? When did you do it? When I was in the loo?"

"You're not a real witch. You hadn't even cast a spell until this year."

"That's hardly my fault."

"You should have stayed with the humans where you belong."

"I take it that you're not really a lawyer then?"

"Of course I'm not. I spend as little time among humans as possible. If I had my way they'd all be wiped out. We could make much better use of their world."

"You really are a piece of work aren't you?"

"Take some advice. Go back to the human world and stay there. You aren't wanted here. There are forces much greater than mine which don't want you here. Do it now while you still can."

She turned and walked away with her skinny sidekick trailing behind.

"Wait! What forces are you talking about? Do you know the Dark One?"

She glanced back over her shoulder and flashed me a chilling smile.

Aunt Lucy insisted we all go back to her house to celebrate. The house was heaving with people—many of whom I'd never even seen before. It seemed that everyone wanted to congratulate me. Everyone except Grandma that was—she was nowhere to be seen. Neither was Lester.

The next morning, a lot of people had very bad hangovers. Fortunately for me, I wasn't one of them. I'd deliberately steered clear of the alcohol.

My phone rang. It was the concierge from Tregar Court. I'd asked him to call me if he saw either Darcy James or Mr Dixon leave the building followed shortly after by the other.

"She left on foot about ten minutes ago," the concierge said. "Dixon's on his way down to the garage now."

"Thanks," I said, grabbing my bag. "Is he definitely alone?"

"Definitely."

"Okay, thanks."

I had to be quick. I cast the spell, and by using all of my focus, managed to land back in Washbridge, right next to my car. The roads were quiet, so it took just over a minute to reach Tregar Court. Had I been quick enough? I was parked opposite the underground garage entrance. After a couple of minutes, I was beginning to think that I'd missed him, but then I saw the barrier rise. Mr Dixon was behind the wheel of a brand new Jaguar. I stayed a couple of cars back in case he spotted me. Darcy James was waiting on the corner of the high street, close to Ever a Wool Moment. She climbed into the passenger seat of the

Jag, and it took a right onto the ring road. I followed for four miles until they pulled into the car park of a motel and diner on the outskirts of the city. I parked just inside the entrance to the car park, and watched through my rear view mirror, as the pair walked arm in arm towards the diner.

I cast the 'invisible' spell, and made my way in after them. There were no more than a dozen customers inside. Dixon and Darcy James were seated in an alcove at the far side of the room. The ten minutes of invisibility I had was more than enough for me to gather all of the evidence I needed.

I got back to my car just before the spell wore off. Everything was starting to make sense now, but if I was going to have a solid case to present to the police, I was going to need Mrs Dixon to fill in the gaps. I had a feeling she'd be only too willing to help.

The concierge caught my eye as I walked through the lobby. "Okay?"

I gave him the thumbs up.

Before I could summon the lift, my phone rang. It was a Candlefield number, but one I didn't recognise.

"Jill Gooder?" a female voice barked.

"Speaking."

"This is Inspector Jewell."

"Oh, hello." Our paths had crossed before. Maxine Jewell hadn't taken kindly to my involvement in the Candlefield Cup case even though I'd managed to solve it. "What can I do for you?"

"I understand you've been poking around the offices of The Candle."

"I'm not sure I'd call it poking around exactly. I was just—"

"Well don't. I've told you before; you have no authority in Candlefield. Stick to serving tea and cakes at the tea room."

"Why is it that no one seems interested in investigating TDO?"

"You don't get to ask the questions. Just stay out of police business if you know what's good for you."

"That sounds like a threat."

"Just do it."

With that, she ended the call. Who had told her that I'd been to the offices of The Candle, and more importantly why? What were they so worried about?

Chapter 26

Mrs Dixon answered the door wearing an apron; her hands were covered in flour. "Oh, hello again."

"You remember me?"

"Of course. I'm afraid Reginald is out."

"It's actually you I wanted to speak to. Can I come in?"

"Err—yes, of course. You caught me in the middle of baking. Reginald loves my fruit scones. Go through to the living room while I wash my hands. Would you like a drink? Tea? Coffee?"

I declined. The news I was about to deliver was probably going to turn Mrs Dixon's world upside down. The sooner I got it over with, the better.

"Right then." Mrs Dixon returned sans apron. "How can I help you?"

"You might want to take a seat."

"Oh dear." She looked genuinely worried now. "What's wrong?"

"Are you aware that your husband and Darcy James are having an affair?"

The colour drained from her face, and I had my answer. "That's ridiculous," she managed at last. "Reginald would never look at another woman."

"I'm afraid it's true. I have evidence." I pulled out my phone. "Can I show you?"

She looked at me with pleading eyes—she didn't want to believe that what I was saying was true. "I suppose so," she said weakly.

I held up the phone, and played back the video I'd recorded earlier in the diner.

"Why did the idiot top himself?" Darcy James said.

"Who knows? Couldn't handle the guilt probably," Dixon said. "Still, he's done us a favour. The police have closed the case now."

"What about that private eye?"

"Don't worry about her. She's got nothing."

Dixon leaned forward and placed a long kiss on Darcy's lips.

"When are you going to tell her?" Darcy said.

"Soon."

"When is soon?"

"We have to be patient. We've come this far. It would be stupid to jeopardise things now."

"But I want to be with you." Darcy put her hand on Dixon's. "I want to spend every moment with you. I can't bear the thought of you touching her. Of you sleeping with her."

"Do you think I want to? I think of you all the time. But we have to be careful."

"I'm sorry I had to show you that," I said.

"I gave him everything," Mrs Dixon said through her tears. "I've never looked at another man."

"Can I ask — ?"

"Would you excuse me?" She didn't wait for an answer — instead, she disappeared in the direction of the bedrooms. How much time did I have before Mr Dixon came back? I was banking on him being otherwise engaged with Darcy for a while, but what if Mrs Dixon had gone into the bedroom to call her husband?

"I'm sorry about that." She returned, looking more self composed.

"I'm sorry you had to find out that way."

She brushed aside my words. "Not your fault. I've known something wasn't right for some time. I just wouldn't let myself believe it."

"I think your husband may have had something to do with Alan Dennis's murder."

"He did."

Her frankness caught me by surprise. "You knew?"

"Of course. What would you like to know?"

Mrs Dixon answered all of my questions and filled in all of the gaps. The Dixons, Darcy James and Jason Allan had all conspired to kill Alan Dennis. Mr Dixon had been the instigator and the brains behind the plan.

"Alan Dennis had recognised Reginald and me," Mrs Dixon said.

"Hardly surprising, seeing as how one of your earlier schemes caused him to go bankrupt, and essentially ruined his life. Had he threatened to expose you?"

"Not as far as I know, but Reginald was sure it was only a matter of time."

"Why didn't you just up sticks and move away like you usually do?"

"We're right in the middle of our latest project."

The way she referred to the Ponzi schemes as 'projects' showed a callous disregard for the devastating effect they had on people's lives. I wanted to shake her, but now wasn't the time.

"If we'd abandoned it," she said, "we'd have been ruined."

"So you decided to kill Dennis."

"I didn't want anything to do with it, but Reginald said it was the only way."

"How did he get Jason Allan to do it?"

"He didn't. Darcy James did that. She was in a relationship with Jason. At least, I thought she was.

Reginald had said she was short of money, and that she'd approached him for a loan. He said that he'd agreed to help her if she would persuade Jason to do it. I suppose that was all a lie."

"It looks that way. I suspect your husband and Darcy were having an affair before she hooked up with Jason. Jason was just the patsy in all of this. But how on earth did Darcy manage to persuade him to kill for her?"

"She told Jason that Alan Dennis had assaulted her and was still stalking her. She told him that she was afraid of Dennis."

"Did you know that Alan Dennis was Jason Allan's father?"

Mrs Dixon's composure melted away again. "What? That can't be true. Jason wouldn't have killed his own father no matter how much he loved Darcy."

"He didn't know — at least not at the time. His father had left his mother before Jason was born. Alan Dennis had been paying Jason's rent, but had never revealed who he was. Jason only found out after he'd killed him. I'm almost certain that's why he committed suicide."

"That poor boy." She took a deep breath. "So what happens now?"

"I'm taking this to the police. I'd like you to come with me."

"What will happen to me?"

"I don't know, but it'll be far worse if you don't tell them everything you know straight away."

I tried to get hold of Maxwell, but reached Sushi. With her usual charm, she agreed to meet Mrs Dixon and me at the police station. I insisted Jack Maxwell be present. She said she'd see what she could do.

By the time I'd finished at the police station and got back to Candlefield, most of the revellers from the night before had made their way back home—many of them still nursing hangovers no doubt. I'd had nothing to eat all morning, and was craving a blueberry muffin.

"Are the twins working in the tea room?" I asked Aunt Lucy.

"Supposedly, but it wouldn't surprise me if they've gone back to bed. They looked terrible when they left here this morning. How do you feel?"

"Me? I'm fine. I didn't have much to drink."

"You did fantastically well yesterday at the Levels. Everyone is really proud of you."

"Except Grandma."

"Including Grandma, but she'll never admit it. You know what she's like."

"I'm beginning to."

"My ears are burning," Grandma said.

How did she creep in like that?

"Morning mother," Aunt Lucy said.

"It smells like a brewery in here."

"We were celebrating last night. You should have joined us."

"Nothing to celebrate. And where's that Fester of yours?"

Aunt Lucy's smile disappeared. "His name is Lester!"

"So where is he? Has he dumped you already?"

"Grandma!" I stepped in.

"Can't I ask a simple question now? The man seems to have disappeared off the face of the earth, and no one seems to know why."

"I don't want to discuss it." Aunt Lucy walked away.

"What about you?" Grandma turned to me. "You were meant to be investigating. Do you know what's happened to him? No one tells me anything."

Is there any wonder?

"I heard that," Grandma said.

Whoops. When would I learn she could hear my thoughts?

It was difficult to say which of the twins looked worse. Amber was behind the cake shop counter with her head propped up on her hand. Pearl was behind the tea room counter—sitting on a stool with her eyes barely open.

"Morning you two," I said as loudly as I could.

"Shhh!"

"Shhh!"

"Oh, I'm sorry. Have you got a hangover?"

They both nodded, but then cringed at the effort.

"How come you look so good?" Amber asked.

"Because I didn't get drunk last night. I've been working in Washbridge all morning. Just solved a case."

"I thought you looked pleased with yourself," Pearl said. "Do you want anything?"

"I'll take a cup of tea and one of your best blueberry muffins, please."

Just then the door opened behind me.

"Jill," Annie Christy said. "I hoped I might catch you here. Could I have a word in private, please?"

"Sure. Do you want a drink or anything?"

"Nothing for me, thanks."

I led the way over to a table for two at the back of the shop. No one would overhear us there. Was she about to slam me for interfering in the family business?

"I wanted to thank you," Annie said. "For keeping this unfortunate business under wraps."

"Your mother has spoken to you then?"

"We had a long talk. I feel so bad about trying to make her sell the business when it was the last thing she wanted to do."

"You were doing it with the best of intentions."

"Maybe, but I should have known, and Mum should have felt she could talk to me about it. I've told the would-be buyer that the bakery is no longer for sale. I just hope that my stupidity hasn't done any long term harm to the business."

"I'm sure it hasn't. If your other customers are anything like the twins, they'll be prepared to cut your mum some slack. After all, her cakes are still the best in Candlefield." I took a bite of the muffin.

"Thanks, Jill. We owe you one. If there's ever anything I can do to help you, please let me know."

Not long after Annie Christy had left, my phone rang. It was another unknown Candlefield number. Someone else warning me off the TDO investigation?

"Jill Gooder?" It was a male voice.

"Speaking."

"I have some information which might interest you. About TDO."

"Who am I speaking to?"

"No names. I used to be a reporter on The Candle."

"Used to be?"

"I can't talk on the phone. Do you know Magpie Place?"

"I can find it."

"Meet me there in ten minutes."

"How will I know – ?"

The line was dead.

Magpie Place was a small courtyard to the north of Candlefield – an area I hadn't been to before. I'd set off immediately the call had ended, but it still took me just under fifteen minutes to get there. All of the streets around the courtyard were narrow – too narrow for cars. It reminded me a little of the Shambles area of York which I'd once visited on a school trip. The courtyard had a bar and restaurant on one side with shops opposite. On the other two sides were offices and houses. The courtyard itself was practically deserted. I glanced around – there were three men – none of whom seemed to be paying me any particular attention. All I could do was wait.

The woman's scream made me jump.

"Help!" she yelled. "Help me."

I followed the others as they went to the woman's aid. She led the way up one of the narrow roads.

"There!" She pointed to a doorway. The two men who'd been in front of me bent down, and I could see that they were attending to a man who was lying on the ground. The pool of blood beneath his head told its own story.

Chapter 27

I had no way of knowing if the man who'd been
murdered in Magpie Place was the same man who'd
contacted me, but it was a pretty safe bet. Someone wasn't
happy about my investigation into TDO, and was
prepared to do anything, including murder, to stop it.

"How's Kathy settling into her new job?" Mrs V asked.
"I haven't heard anything from her in a couple of days,
but something tells me Grandma isn't going to be fun to
work for."
"Is she ever fun?"
"Not really. What time is Jackie Langford due here?"
"In a few minutes."

Winky looked particularly pleased with himself—never a
good sign.
"Here!" He pushed a glossy brochure across the desk to
me.
"What's this?"
"It's the offices I told you about. They're a really high
spec. We might even get decent broadband over there."
I would have told him where he could stuff his brochure,
but I didn't want him to create a scene while Jackie
Langford was in the office. "I'll take a look later. I have a
client due any minute."
He one-eyed me suspiciously. Fortunately, before he
could say anything, Mrs V opened the door and showed
Jackie Langford inside.
Winky wrapped himself around her legs as she stroked
him. They really were BFFs.

"You said you had news," she said as she joined me at my desk.

I laid out the story as I knew it. "It's a tragedy from beginning to end. Jason had no idea that Alan Dennis was his father. When he found out, he was devastated."

"And took his own life."

I nodded. "Alan recognised the Dixons. Hardly surprising given the circumstances. Whether he'd intended to do anything about it we'll never know, but Reginald Dixon wasn't taking any chances."

"What about the CCTV?"

"I'm not sure we'll ever know the full details, but my guess is that Darcy James had tried to persuade Jason Allan to kill Alan. He'd wanted to help her, but had been too afraid. Darcy needed to persuade him he could commit the crime without fear of being caught. That's when she hatched the plan to stage the scene for the CCTV and to swap the tapes. She's a woman who knows how to use her considerable charms to get what she wants from men. Hooking up with Tony, the man at Gravesend Security, had been easy for her. He was putty in her hands. Once he'd agreed to swap the tapes, she'd been able to convince Jason that he'd have nothing to fear. The three of them in the lift: the Dixons and Darcy James had choreographed the thing perfectly. By dressing identically on both days, they'd made it almost impossible to spot the difference between the CCTV recordings."

"Why didn't the Dixons simply leave Washbridge when they recognised Alan?"

"Mrs Dixon said it was because they were in the midst of a new Ponzi scheme, but I don't buy that. Reginald Dixon probably told his wife that, but I'm more inclined to believe he didn't want to risk losing Darcy James. If they'd had to relocate and find new identities, that would have put an end to the affair."

"What's going to happen to them?"

"Difficult to say. They'll definitely all be charged with conspiracy to murder, but because they were actually present when the murder took place, they may even be charged with murder. Mrs Dixon may get away with the lesser charge if she agrees to appear as a witness for the prosecution."

"Will she do that?"

"I'm certain she will. She loved her husband and had stood by him all of those years only to be traded in for a younger model. She wants her revenge."

Fortunately for me, Winky was asleep when Jackie Langford left, so I was able to sneak out before he could start on at me again about moving offices.

"Are we relocating, Jill?" Mrs V asked as I was leaving.

"No. Why?"

"Someone put this brochure on my desk." She held up an identical brochure to the one Winky had foisted upon me.

"We're not going anywhere. I love this old office."

I'd put it off as long as I could, but it was time to confront Miles Best. What exactly was I supposed to say to him? I had absolutely no idea. I was en route when I bumped into Lester — literally.

"Jill?"

"Where have you been hiding?"

"I haven't."

"Come on. No one's seen you for ages. When I saw you the other day, you ran off. Aunt Lucy is terribly upset."

"That's the last thing I wanted."

"What did you expect? You disappeared without a word."

"I thought if I stayed away, she might just forget about me."

"Really? Don't you realise how much she cares about you? She's not going to forget about you just like that. If you've found someone else or grown tired of the relationship, the least you can do is tell her."

"No. It's nothing like that."

"Then what is it?"

"I can't say."

"I'm not leaving until you do."

He could see I meant what I said, so we found a quiet little coffee shop where he told me everything.

Miles had moved back in with his parents. He'd lived and worked for many years in the human world, but according to the twins, had grown tired of that life so had moved back to Candlefield. Just as the twins had said, he lived on a small cul-de-sac, but I didn't know which house was his, so I asked the young witch who was tending to her garden.

"Excuse me. I'm looking for Miles Best."

"What do you want him for?" she said, abruptly. "Are you his girlfriend?"

"No. Nothing like that. Do you know him?"

"I should do. I've lived here all my life. This used to be my parents' house. They're both dead now."

"I'm sorry."

"Miles and I grew up together. We played together and

went to school together. I always thought—" She seemed to drift off—lost in her own thoughts for a few seconds.

"I didn't catch your name," I said.

"It's Mindy. Mindy Lowe."

It didn't take a private investigator to see that Mindy Lowe had a thing for Miles.

"I understand he came back recently. Has he changed much?"

"Not to me. He might look a little different, I guess, but don't we all?" She laughed nervously.

"Have you seen much of him since he moved back to Candlefield?"

She shook her head. "We've said hello. That's all."

"Which is his house?"

She pointed. "Tell him I said 'hi' would you?"

"Sure."

Miles answered the door. "It's you, again. I saw you in Cuppy C with Amber and Pearl."

"That's right. Are your parents in?"

"No, they've gone shopping. Why?"

"I'd like a word with you. Can I come in?" I didn't wait for an answer.

"I thought the twins liked me," Miles said.

I felt like I'd just kicked a puppy.

"They do like you, Miles," I lied. "But they're both engaged now. How would it look if they were to be seen with you? I'm sure you understand. And besides, their fiancés are big guys. Very big."

"Really?"

"You wouldn't want to upset them."

"No. I don't want to do that. I had no idea."

"Oh, and by the way, Mindy says 'hi'."

"She did?" He smiled. "Mindy and I have been friends forever."

"You do realise she'd like to be more than just friends, don't you?"

"Mindy? No. She doesn't think of me like that."

Were all men this stupid? On the evidence so far, I'd have to say yes.

"You're wrong. Trust me on this one. Why don't you invite her over for a cup of tea and a chat?" I grinned. "I'm sure she'll say yes."

"Really? You're sure?"

"One hundred percent."

I let the twins know that they were off the hook with Miles, but declined their offer of a free blueberry muffin. My jeans were already pinching a little. En route to Aunt Lucy's I made a phone call to Annie Christy.

"Annie? It's Jill. You know you said I should call if I ever needed a favour? Well—"

Aunt Lucy cried when I explained the situation.

"The stupid idiot."

"He was afraid to tell you."

"Why?"

"Men are stupid. He thought you'd think less of him because he'd lost his magic powers."

"I couldn't care less about that."

"*I* know that, and *you* know that. But Lester—well—Lester is a man."

"I have to go and talk to him."

"Before you do—I took the liberty of speaking to Annie

Christy, Beryl's daughter. She works for SupAid, a charity which works with sups who have lost their powers. She said that she'd be happy to put Lester in touch with the right people. According to her, the problem often turns out to be only a temporary one, so his powers may yet return. But if they don't, there is support available."

"Thanks, Jill. I'll make sure he contacts her." She opened her arms. "Come here, and give me a hug."

I left Aunt Lucy's and started to walk towards the town square. It was market day, and I thought I'd spend an hour looking around. My phone rang.

"Jill? It's Jack Maxwell."

"Hello, Detective Maxwell."

"Detective?" He laughed. "I guess I deserve that. Look, I have some news I thought you'd like to hear."

"About the Tregar case?"

"No, I think you know all there is to know about that. I just wanted you to know that Susan Shay has gone back to her old post. Things didn't work out for her down here."

"That is a shame. Just when me and Sushi were beginning to hit it off."

"She's a good detective."

"Yeah, so you said."

"Anyway, I just thought you would want to know."

"Thanks."

"Okay."

"Okay."

"Bye, then."

"Bye, Jack."

Yes! So long, Sushi! Now that she was out of the picture maybe Jack and me could give it another go. Whatever 'it' was. It's not like I had the added complication of Drake to worry about.

"Are you Jill Gooder?" The scruffy looking wizard stepped out of a doorway in front of me.
"Who are you? What do you want?" I was on my guard — ready with the 'lightning bolt' spell if I needed it.
"I'm Raven, Drake's brother."
"Drake? Did he send you to see me?"
"No. He doesn't know I'm here."
"Is he okay?"
"Yes, well sort of. He's not happy that you dumped him. You found out about his record, didn't you? Did Daze tell you?"
"I — err"
"Never mind. I know it was her. There's more to it than she knows."
"What do you mean?"
"Drake did nothing wrong. He took the blame and the fall for me. He should never have been arrested or convicted. I wanted to say something at the time, but he wouldn't let me. Whatever you think he did, he didn't. He's a good man, and a fantastic brother. If it wasn't for him, I'd probably be dead by now. I just thought you should know."
With that, he turned and left.
Oh bum! What had I done? I'd treated Drake badly, and hadn't even given him a chance to put his side of the story. What was I supposed to do now? There was only one thing I could do at a time like this.

"Thanks." I took three custard creams from the newly

opened packet.

"Are you sure you've got enough there?" Kathy said.

"Go on then. I'll have one more."

She snatched the packet away before I had the chance.

"I really needed this." I took a bite of custard cream nirvana. "I've had one heck of a day."

"You think you've had a bad day. You should have been here this morning."

"Why what happened?"

"Lizzie was inconsolable. I didn't think I was going to get her to school."

"Is she under the weather?"

"No, nothing like that. Do you remember that scrawny old soft toy?"

"She has so many."

"The singing rabbit."

"Oh yeah. What did you call it? *Things*?"

"Yeah. Well, we had no choice but to throw him out."

"Why?"

"Things fell apart."

"Can't you mend him?"

"I've tried, but the whole thing has perished. There's nothing left to fix. Pete's going to have a look around town after work to see if he can find anything similar. I'm not sure it will make any difference even if he does. It still won't be 'Things'."

Poor Lizzie.

There was a white envelope waiting for me back at my flat.

On my coffee table!

How had it got there? I checked every room and the

garden, but there was no sign of anyone. The doors were still locked, and there was no sign of forced entry through a window. I hated this—the thought that someone could have gained entry to the one place where I should feel secure.

The envelope had not been addressed, it simply bore my name. Inside was a card with a single word on the front: 'Congratulations'. It wasn't signed, but inside someone had written: '*Congratulations on your level two win*'.

Below those words was a hand-drawn picture of a bird—a magpie. The bird was standing in a pool of blood.

BOOKS BY ADELE ABBOTT

Witch P.I. Mysteries:
Witch Is When It All Began
Witch Is When Life Got Complicated
Witch Is When Everything Went Crazy
Witch Is When Things Fell Apart
Witch Is When The Bubble Burst

Ghost Hunter Librarian Mysteries:
Coming in 2016

AUTHOR'S WEB SITE
http:www.AdeleAbbott.com

FACEBOOK
http://www.facebook.com/AdeleAbbottAuthor

MAILING LIST
(new release notifications only)
http:/AdeleAbbott.com/adele/new-releases/

Printed in Great Britain
by Amazon